City of Anarchy

Miguel Olmedo

First Edition

PAGE PUBLISHING
Conneaut Lake, PA

First originally published by Page Publishing 2023

ISBN 979-8-88960-266-8 (pbk)
ISBN 979-8-88960-293-4 (digital)

Printed in the United States of America

Dedicated to Juan Francisco Crespo, my grandfather, my abuelo, our viejo.

Contents

Preface

This book is intended to make the reader question if it is possible to live in a world after an apocalypse, not the world that will be but the world that might be. This book is told from the perspective of a very lost man in a very dystopian city of violence, revolution, and madness. The characters in this story are trying to live somewhat of a normal life despite living a very broken world. They pray that one day they will be saved from the bondages of oppression from a tyrannical leader who abuses her power. The evil government nicknamed the State has been committing crimes against its citizens, with manhunts, vehicles being searched, houses being searched without warrants, and finally, leaders who got away with their crimes with impunity. Even if the people may succeed in defeating this dictatorship, and even if one nightmare may have ended, another may have just begun!

City of Anarchy

Chapter 1

The Bartons

Smart City was filled with so much evil sometimes fresh corpses were found in the street from innocent victims who were tortured and killed by the State for unknown reasons. And to the top it all off, a new drug called Flakka was legalized by them also. This drug has a frozen effect in the brain, which can make any poor chump mentally ill for life. Nobody seems to care, except the Bartons.

Sarah Barton was trying to do some good in a corrupt system. She realized going inside too deep could mean death. She bragged that she was one of the best members of an underground organization called the resistance even though she worked with more experienced people like herself. Her husband, Patrick Barton, was a psychologist who worked in a psychiatric hospital called Life's Garden Hospital until he began trying to help me at Blackstone Penitentiary. Over time, Patrick's professional nature sort of cracked. He was warned by the warden, if he had one more outburst at work, he would be fired.

Every night, Patrick and Sarah went to bed, thinking of the hard times they had, living in this city. One night, Sarah heard a group of people knocking loudly at the door at midnight outside the house. She became enraged and began yelling at the group, who began to knock on the door even louder. It was the State, the ones responsible for turning Smart City into a living nightmare.

They explained to her that she must pay up her money to the State, saying, "If you don't come back within a week or two, we will take up your property and sell it to another."

Sarah was nervous yet at the same time furious with them, so she simply said, "Get the hell out of here."

Then they slapped her in the cheek. She tried to fight back, but then all of them pointed at her with their own guns.

One of them said to her with a stern voice, "Go back!"

"All right, all right."

"It's a good thing that all you little creatures can't afford even a single weapon."

Then they left while laughing about what just happened. While going back into her bedroom, Patrick woke up.

"You were awake this whole time?" said Sarah.

"I'm so sorry, honey. Things have just gotten crazy these days."

Sarah sighed, trying to not to react about any stress or anguish; so instead of getting upset, she said, "I know, honey, but we can't do anything."

Her husband replied, "I understand that, sweetheart, but how dare they make us live like slaves?"

"We won't live like slaves unless we see it that way," explained Sarah.

"Sarah, stop!" yelled Patrick.

Sarah became enraged. "What? You think I don't want to have a normal life. You think I don't want to sometimes just die? I worked with the resistance to this disgusting phase until I realized it was just a way of life. I hate this life, Patrick, but there's… Sorry… I'm so sorry."

Patrick sighed and said, "Okay. If they come back next week, Sarah, just take a deep breath because you're not alone in this."

"Well, maybe you're right." Sarah sighed. "Hey, at least they weren't the neighbor's dogs."

In that moment, it was a rare time for Patrick and Sarah to embrace each other and even chuckle a bit; they hadn't been talking to each other since the governor of Smart City had resigned.

Believing you don't have a choice was one thing, but another when you really didn't have a choice.

Chapter 2

Nabeel Toameh

The next day, Patrick was home when the phone rang.

"Hello," said Patrick.

"Patrick, it's me."

Patrick was surprised and confused when the man spoke on the phone. He replied, "Who is this?"

"It's your father's ghost."

"What?" Patrick exclaimed.

"Heh, I'm just playing with you. It's me, Toameh."

"A sense of humor from you. That's new."

"Look, I know it's a weekend, but some of my doctors aren't working well with the patients. Can you fill in?"

"Warden, I snapped at a patient the last time you asked me to come in. Why are you asking again?" queried Patrick.

"Well, some of the other doctors are actually worse than you," said Toameh.

"You fired them, didn't you?" questioned Patrick.

"What do you think, Doctor?"

"I think there's more information to what you are saying, sir."

"Are you going to come in or what?"

"Maybe, but first, how are you doing?"

"Just fine. A patient just bit me in the hand a few hours ago," replied Toameh sarcastically.

"Oh, I hope you're okay. Look, I'm coming," said Patrick.

Patrick drove off in his Lincoln Navigator. He was thinking about the director. He seemed like a nice guy, with sometimes a very quiet voice, and knew a lot of the Bartons, even their secrets and personal secrets.

While at the hospital, Toameh saw Patrick and yelled, "Hurry! Hurry! A patient is in crisis."

The patient was a kid who seemed to be eight or seven years old and was running upstairs. Patrick and Toameh chased him. They were able to corner the kid. Toameh restrained him so Patrick could use the syringe with a loud of anesthesia inside. It slowly began to take effect, and then the kid was asleep.

Patrick said, "Jesus Christ, boss, I thought all the patients guard with them."

"They do," said Toameh.

"Then still why can some kid just wake up out of nowhere with nobody to watch him?"

"Patrick, I can explain."

"Then tell me. I could have been at home right now."

"Patrick. The hospital is compromised," said Toameh.

"What? Why?"

"Because of the State."

Toameh explained that Life's Garden Hospital was supposed to be a place for adults and children. In an interrogation room inside the statehouse, they accused Toameh that one of the children was not mentally ill but infected with Flakka. Toameh explained that it was outrageous and that his patients were all mentally ill, not medically sick, but they would not listen. They threatened him by saying, "If you want both your patients and your hospital to keep going, give us the brat!"

Toameh refused to go along with it; so the State decided that they would shut down his business as director of the hospital. The next thing he did was, he fired all his guards and doctors and explained to them the same way he was explaining to Patrick. It would be one of the hardest things he had ever done.

Patrick was surprised by Toameh's statement and said, "So you told me to come here just to fire me, right?"

"I don't know."

Patrick always knew they had no police, no hope, and nothing to fix this world from what the State did or what their number one drug was doing to this world. Patrick wished things could be different and find another job, but he knew this was the only working place that he could find.

Patrick said, "Are you going to send that kid to the State?"

"Maybe... I don't know," said Toameh.

"I want to make sure the kid is okay."

Toameh was a bit nervous because they could come in any moment. But he decided one last time was fine.

Patrick saw him, and the kid was beginning to wake up. He had a straitjacket and was struggling to break out.

"Easy, easy, it's all right!" said Patrick.

"Who are you?" asked the kid.

Patrick explained that he was a doctor who worked with patients to sort out their problems and find solutions. He also explained to him that he blacked out, and he wanted to talk to him about it.

"Oh yeah?" said the kid.

Patrick asked him for his name. He told him it was Jacob Bordeaux, or JB for short. Patrick asked JB how he arrived here. JB didn't want to tell Patrick because he was afraid Patrick would tell the State. Patrick made a lie by saying that this was a private place, and what they would talk about was confidential.

"No, I'm sorry, Doc," said JB.

This wasn't the first time Patrick met a patient like this. A long time ago, Dr. Patrick Harding Barton was once a medical doctor that switched careers to become a college professor in psychology at St Louis University. He was fascinated with cases with the mind and wanted to find an antidote to help those suffering from Flakka. He secretly worked in his basement, finding out what triggered it. He believed it was a chemical imbalance in the amygdala, which was the center for emotions, emotional behavior, and motivation. So he tried to encourage the positive side of the mind and segregate the negative, but for so long, all tests had failed; but Patrick was still working on an antidote to this day.

After nineteen minutes of talking with JB, Patrick went to his boss.

Nabeel was thinking about what Patrick had told him early about Flakka and JB being infected. Nabeel asked Patrick if everything was okay with the boy.

"He's calming down," said Patrick.

Nabeel told Patrick that his wife, Sarah, had called while he was helping JB. Patrick called Sarah to find out what was going on. Patrick was a little nervous because of the environment and the state of the city. So while calling Sarah, he decided to tell her a joke while on the phone.

He said, "Knock, knock."

"Who's there?"

"Interrupting cow."

"Interrupting…oh god!"

"Moo!"

Then they both laughed. But even with happy moments, the dark moments were always stronger when the State was in charge!

Chapter 3

The Rebels

Sarah Barton headed out to a meeting with her boss, Mark Talbot, the leader of the resistance. Mark was an intelligent man, with a lot of hate for corruption, and trusted only a few people. Sarah was one of them. Sarah met up with two other good rebel members, Louis Jackson and Wilfred McNally. Talbot knew that these individuals couldn't be corrupted or would give in.

Talbot told the three groups—Sarah Barton, Louis Jackson, and Wilfred McNally—to go to his office.

Then McNally said out of nowhere, "We better be careful, guys, because the old man might snap at us again." (He was referring to Talbot.)

Then everybody in the resistance laughed, except Jackson, Barton, and epically Talbot.

"Shut your Mouths and get back to work!" Talbot said to his group.

"And, McNally, stop making an ass out of yourself."

"Which one, the donkey or the asshole" McNally replied.

Talbot answered, "Yes."

Now behind closed doors, Talbot told the three rebels that this meeting was confidential, and he didn't want some of his men or women to know because some were just a bunch of cowards and only just got here because of the system.

He then explained that none of them would be able to tell their spouses or family members. Talbot would tell them when necessary.

This made the three of them very nervous and wondered, *Why is it so secretive?*

Then Sarah asked Talbot, "Boss, what mission are we enlisting?"

Talbot answered, "It is technically…an illegal operation. It has something against the State."

They were all shocked by his statement and questioned that he might have lost his mind.

"Boss, the last time we fought, it did not end well," said Jackson.

Talbot responded, "Look, I know, but we can't just do small crap, like cleaning the streets and playing hero when someone needs help. Look…it wasn't always like this. This world needs to be free of them treating us as their slaves, okay? We need to do more."

Jackson asked, "Yeah, how?"

Sarah came up with the idea of being an undercover spy. Everyone laughed.

Jackson asked, "That's exactly what we did the last time. Remember what happened to John Clay?"

"Clay was an idiot to do it alone, but we have a chance to do it all in three people," Talbot replied.

"What do you mean?" said McNally.

Talbot jumped in, "Seriously, McNally, the laws of both Smart City and this country are to be protected, but because of a few, it's now practically impossible to solve serious crimes. Even minor crimes can be difficult to stop sometimes. Hey, I thought you were for the resistance."

"Yeah," said McNally. "But I'm only here to clean up graffiti and stop murderers, thieves, and rapists, not take on an entire system!"

And Talbot said, "Then get out!"

Everyone was stunned when Talbot yelled at McNally. Even Sarah and Jackson could see Talbot's face looking red as blood; and McNally was so shocked by Talbot's outburst he became pale his face was white as snow, but about a few seconds after, he finally stood up to him and stuttered, "W…with pleasure!"

Talbot was speechless. McNally saw that Talbot was shocked, so he took advantage of his boss' reaction and spat on his desk and said, "Bye, boss."

In that moment, McNally decided that his job in the resistance was not for him. He got up and went outside while inside McNally was chased by Sarah, and she tried to convince him to stay.

McNally said, "Barton, I might be crazy, but I'm not stupid."

"If you leave, you will be stupid," said Sarah.

"What are you talking about? If you do this, you'll never see your husband again…" said McNally.

Sarah responded, "Yeah? If I don't do this, those bastards might go to my house again and try to ruin both me and my husband's lives even worse. I can't take this anymore. If I'm going to be a hero, I'm going to be a damn good one."

McNally looked at Sarah with a long face. I knew McNally a while back, and I also know that he was not a coward; he was worried because this operation seemed doomed even before it started. He was worried that it wouldn't be able to clean up Smart City and make things even worse for the people in it. But about a few minutes after, McNally looked straight to accept to Sarah's eyes and saw a brave and confident spirit.

He told her, "Aw, the hell with it."

She smiled and went with her inside, and McNally apologized to Talbot, but he warned that if he spat on his desk again that he was done, so the four began making their case to overthrow Linda Smith, the leader of the State. It wouldn't be easy to take her on because her father, the late philanthropist and one of the richest men in America, had gotten both him and his family immunity for any acts of criminal activities anywhere.

McNally said, "It's not going to be easy, but there is a better way to overthrow her."

"What are you suggesting?" said Talbot.

"Why not just take her?"

Sarah started to laugh and thought McNally was joking only to realize both McNally and Talbot were considering it.

"You both can't be serious, can you?" said Sarah.

"Yeah, well, sometimes you have to know how it goes in this city of anarchy," said Talbot.

Chapter 4

LINDA SMITH

Talbot told the undercover group his plan of action. He wanted Linda Smith taken into custody. The problem was that Linda Smith had diplomatic immunity and had the legal freedom to do whatever she wanted. Linda Smith didn't have to answer to anyone—not the cops, not the military, not the supreme court, not even God

Talbot instructed the group to find Smith and bring her to the station! Sarah, McNally, and Jackson nodded in agreement. Sarah suggested that they wear a bulletproof vest underneath as she knew how dangerous the State was. The chief agreed.

Talbot knew that they would need an extra rebel for this mission to be successful. He knew he needed someone who could be trusted for this top-secret undercover operation. He decided to send a man by the name of Jose Mendez to do the job.

The goal was to help the three undercover rebels enter Smith's senate. The three undercover rebels would stage a fight with Mendez outside the senate. All this fighting would attract the attention of a senator. Hopefully, this fight would allow Sarah, McNally, and Jackson a chance to join the senator.

Two days later, the group carried out their plan. The fight attracted the attention of a senator inside the statehouse. During the fight, the same senator shot Mendez in the chest, but his vest protected him. McNally, Jackson, and Sarah were part of the fight with Mendez.

Jackson stepped in and said to the group gathered outside, "Don't worry. I'll take care of him."

Jackson gave Mendez a nod, who nodded back, and gave him a punch so hard he was on the floor, unconscious. The undercover group turned to the senator and asked what they should do with Mendez. A senator suggested they carry him into the safe house and lock him up in the basement, with other cops they had previously captured.

The three agreed. They were surprised that there were other rebels locked in the basement.

Sarah asked the senator, "What's your name?"

The senator laughed and said, "Linda Smith."

They were surprised to hear that name, who was responsible for destroying this world; and to make it more shocking, they were seeing that person right there who claimed to be Linda Smith, the one who everyone thought would be our greatest leader and healer for the world but instead was our greatest enemy and cancer to the world. McNally, Jackson, and Sarah walked into the State senate, with the lady who claimed to be Linda Smith. The department was a large black house, with a huge flag next to it that had an upside-down triangle in red, white, and black, with a lightning-like S in the middle. The State senate was once a group home until a mysterious virus came and killed countless lives. That's when Smith came to power, claiming she wanted peace, but eventually grew more power-hungry and deceived us and broke every promise of a better future.

While in the statehouse, Smith called for one of her doctors to examine the three of us if we had any injuries that needed to be patched up.

The doctor said to her, "Linda, there's really no serious injuries."

But before he had time to explain to her, she was already in a meeting with other members while Jackson went up and knocked out the doctor in the face. Sarah looked shocked while McNally looked delighted.

"What the hell was that, Jackson?"

"What, was he going to snitch?" said Jackson.

McNally then looked down and said, "That was such a badass man."

Smith called for ten associates, twenty soldiers, and three doctors to discuss business. McNally, Jackson, and Sarah were included while the third doctor, who had realized the three undercover cops didn't have any wounds and was about to expose them, was quickly knocked unconscious by Sarah and had put him in a closet.

While Smith was explaining her plans, McNally, Jackson, and Barton took the doctor's unconscious body and put him next to a corner covered with multiple objects. They then decided to follow Smith, and while following her, they were in a meeting that looked like the house of representatives at Washington. The three of them watched and took in every move and word. While Smith was addressing the group, one of her senators got suspicious and asked about the three people in the back. He had never seen them before and wanted to know who they were.

Smith was annoyed. She said, "They're one of us!"

The senator said, "How can they be one of us since I've never seen them before?"

Smith got mad. She rushed to the senator, grabbed him, and slammed his head to the desk and said, "You don't question me… EVER!"

"Yes, yes…"

And Smith said, "What did you say? Yes, what?"

"Yes, Madame Smith! Yes, Madame Smith!"

Linda said, "Better! If I see even a glimpse of you questioning me, you will be dead on arrival, got it?"

"Yes, Madame Smith! Yes, Madame Smith!"

Smith continued with her speech. She talked about her dad, the one person who had started this whole operation.

Sixteen years ago

Linda Joan Smith was the illegitimate daughter of a banker named Sal Smith, a man that was both cold and cruel, but at the same time, he wasn't always such a tyrant. Sal had a family that were bankers, who made trillions of dollars and were very much despicable people. Unlike them, Sal was a humanitarian, who loved what he did and never put himself first. He thought that would never change. Until he did when he became governor of Smart City. As time passed, he got connected with other corrupt bankers that used him as a puppet. Then he gradually became more and more corrupt.

During this time, a third war came because of a conflict between both nations of America and Russia. His illegitimate daughter, who was the daughter of a prostitute, became a senator, running for President; her surname then was Drake. Before having the last name Smith, Linda Albert lived in an orphanage, where she was mistreated and beaten by the people there. She was given the name Albert by her adopted parents, Leo and Morgan Drake, who were sent by Sal so he could keep an eye on her until she grew up. Until she was running for president, Leo and Morgan told the truth. Linda was devastated and started to become the coldhearted bastard her father was. Before meeting her father, Linda had a mental breakdown with her adopted parents. She grabbed a kitchen knife and sliced their throats.

The next day, she met her father, covered in blood, and hugged him like a lost child would do. After a few seconds, a mysterious virus came to the world and wiped out half of humanity After the country was nearly destroyed, Smith decided to take power when everyone was desperate for a global leader and a global world government. She decided to become that global leader. She was elected by multiple candidates to make it look like he killed himself. His name was Senator Stanley Clay, the father of John Clay. When she became the leader of the world, families began to suffer under the Smith rule. All of them were still alive, except Sal Smith, who was officially killed by John Clay, who mistakenly believed that it was Sal and not Linda who killed his father, who was executed for treason, and his death crippled the resistance from having another undercover rebel…until now.

Chapter 5

MARK TALBOT

Sarah, McNally, and Jackson left the statehouse after the meeting.

They saw some ways to stop Smith and her senators. Sarah texted Mendez, telling him they would get him out of the basement. Sarah was worried that the State would kill him.

He texted back, "GET ME OUT OF HERE!" Mendez saw a bunch of skeletons scattered all over the basement, and to add insult to injury, the skeletons were all dead cops, and Jose feared he was next.

Sarah, McNally, and Jackson realized they couldn't abandon him, but they also couldn't go back to the station because they were afraid they might be followed by the same senator who was suspicious about them. They texted Talbot.

Sarah wrote, "Boss, we got in, but we weren't able to capture Smith."

"All right, but did you find any useful information?"

"We found out she's crazy."

Talbot chuckled and said, "Well, duh, but anyway, do you know where Mendez is?"

Sarah told the chief, "Mendez is locked in Smith's basement."

"Jesus Christ! Okay, everybody goes home until we find a way to save Mendez and get Smith!"

Sarah Responded, "We can't just leave him since God knows what they might do to him."

"I'm sorry, Sarah."

"No, this isn't right!"

"Do you want me to tell your husband you blew your cover, got killed, and ruined this whole operation? Sarah, for success to happen, sometimes you need to make hard choices. You of all people should know that."

After the mission was completed, Sarah went home to her husband, Patrick, who was on the phone with Talbot about his wife. Sarah went up to Patrick and told him that she was fine and didn't even receive a scratch. Patrick was relieved and hugged his wife.

Patrick said, "Let's relax and watch some television."

"No," Sarah answered. "Let me take a shower."

"Can I go with you?" asked Patrick.

Sarah chuckled and said, "Of course, honey."

The two went upstairs to the bathroom, took their clothes off, and turned the water on. Patrick noticed Sarah's previous bullet wounds on her back. Sarah noticed bite marks on Patrick's right arm, back at Life's Garden Hospital. They had each experienced pain from their jobs. The two embraced and kissed each other. Sarah thought to herself, *I hate the job, but I love the man*, while Patrick thought, *I hate the work, but I'll always love this woman.*

Suddenly they heard noises from downstairs. Sarah went to check it out, only to find out that it was the State, shooting their house from the outside. Sarah became angry.

"I'm going to kill those red-jumpsuit-wearing bastards!" She puts on a few clothes then grabbed her pistol. Patrick tried to stop her by reminding her that she was undercover. Sarah questioned, "How did you know?"

"Because Talbot told me that they would come in any minute and to keep my eye."

"Patrick, those people threw away our lives. If I can at least just take out one of those ugly redheads, I'll save democracy."

Patrick explained, "Look, Sarah, killing one of them won't stop."

"Then what would?"

"Being undercover!"

Sarah and Patrick then saw members of the State leave their house. Sarah realized just killing one senator at their doorstep wouldn't solve anything. It would just blow her cover. Sarah put her pistol back, went to the kitchen, and got herself a couple of flasks. After a couple of sips, she cooled off.

She told Patrick, "I'm sorry."

"Don't be," said Patrick.

The next morning, Sarah got up early, disguised in her red jumpsuit so she could infiltrate the statehouse. She kissed Patrick goodbye and drove off. When she arrived, she parked her car and checked her pistol. When she went inside, she witnessed a fight between two senators. A group of people were encouraging them to fight. McNally and Jackson were in the crowd. Senators were betting money on who would win. A bunch of hundred-dollar bills were drowned on different sides.

One of the fighters cracked the other guy's neck. Sarah's face turned pale when she realized McNally and Jackson would have to fight next. Everyone was yelling for another fight. Sarah couldn't let this happen. She was in a tough spot because, if she interfered, her cover would be blown and she would be shot and killed. Sarah thought about Patrick and what would happen to him if she died. McNally and Jackson took off their jumpsuits, leaving only their underwear, gloves, and boots. The crowd was becoming a circus when they were punching and wrestling and constantly turning the fight into a bloodbath. Sarah was freaking out; she was worried that either McNally or Jackson would be killed. Smith then came out and yelled to the entire senate to stop. She told them that they were going to break in somewhere that opposed them. She wanted to know if they were in or out. They all yelled, "In!" The senators filed out. Jackson stayed back to help save Mendez, who was locked in the basement, while Barton and McNally played along with the break-in.

Chapter 6

EXPOSED!

Sarah and McNally were forced to go along with a break-in to someone who was against Smith, but both had no idea whose house it was. They saw grenades wrapped up inside Smith's tank. Sarah was wondering what kind of mess she and McNally had gotten themselves into when they arrived at the house, but when they arrived, Sarah couldn't see because the senators were crowding the place. Even with a tank in the way, there was no way she could know whose house it was. But Sarah could see a glimpse of the house and realized to her shocking discovery that it was indeed her house, and her husband was indeed inside. The senators barged inside.

They all yelled like animals, speaking at the same time, yelling, "Who's the manager! Who's the manager!"

The senators went on, talking trash, trying to scare anyone inside for not giving in to Smith and the State. They finally found Patrick and were about to jump on the poor guy. About multiple senators were beating and brutalizing him. Sarah could hear Patrick yelling, "Why are you doing this to us?"

"Because you won't pay, peasant!" said Smith.

While on the floor, Smith was holding a Magnum in her hand and was aiming at his head. "No, please don't do it!" said Patrick.

"Goodbye!"

But when she was about to shoot him, three senators fell to the ground by a bullet to the head.

Smith went berserk on one of her senators, asking who pulled the trigger.

Patrick rushed to grab one of the senators' guns from their pockets. She aimed the gun at Smith; but before she could take a shot, one of Smith's men took a shot at Patrick in the knee, who was bleeding, with his body on the floor. Sarah and McNally were shocked and horrified to see Patrick liked that. Sarah saw the whole thing and went off the tank.

McNally yelled, "What the hell do you think you're doing?"

"Saving my husband!" said Sarah.

While doing so, Sarah rushed into the house while McNally stayed inside the tank, and Smith and the senators came inside the tank. The senators threw the grenade at the house while Sarah and Patrick were inside. Unfortunately, no one seemed to have been able to escape the fire. Thick smoke clouds covered the whole room. People were screaming and crying, trying to get out, and none could get out because of the fire.

On the way back to the crib, everyone was inside the tank. McNally saw the evil look in Smith's eyes she described as red eyes from hell.

When the driver brought all of them back, Smith was suspicious if one of her senators shot each other.

While thinking about it, McNally had received a text. He checked his phone, and to his surprise, it said, "We made it out!"

McNally closed his eyes and smiled and said to himself, "Thank God!"

Another text said, "I'm coming back!"

Smith asked those next to her, "Who was it that pulled the trigger?"

The senators told their boss they didn't know. But the same senator who was suspicious about Sarah, McNally, and Jackson was smiling at both as if he knew, when they got back, all hell would break loose.

"We'll find out. I think there's a traitor in here, and I'm going to find out who it is."

While returning to the statehouse, Jackson came up from the basement with Officer Mendez and saw and tried to find a closet to hide them in before Smith and the two undercover rebels came back.

Jackson texted McNally on his phone, saying, "Got Mendez!"

McNally texted back, saying, "Good!"

"How is the mission?"

"We were in the vault, grabbing and looking for the manager, until shots rang off."

"Who did it?"

"I did."

Jackson then heard footsteps coming near the closet and knew things were about to get hairy. Jackson texted, "Call Talbot to get backup!" Then one of the doors was opening. Jackson did the sign of the cross, saying, "My god!" and the door was opened.

Fifteen minutes later, Smith was in a fiery rage and explained that she believed who tried to sabotage the mission.

The same senator who was suspicious of Sarah and McNally played dumb by saying, "What do you mean, madame?"

"Don't call me madame."

All of them denied betraying her.

"Well, if you're so loyal, then you'll die loyal until I find who betrayed me!"

Then she grabbed a Magnum and pointed at her senators. She shot them one by one, hoping that one of them would confess to being a traitor.

The same senator who was suspicious of Sarah and McNally pointed at them, yelling, "It's them. It's them!"

Smith turned her head in confusion, saying, "Thank you," and shot the bastard's brains out. "But you should have told me that before. So this is the thanks for giving you the world."

Sarah informed them that they had no place to go.

Smith laughed and said, "Yeah, right. I own both you and this nation while having diplomatic immunity, so you should have a place to go."

Sarah answered, "Your new order is finished!"

"And your kind is extinct."

Then the three of them were suddenly in a Mexican standoff, with their guns pointed at each other.

Smith then smiled, saying, "You know those two undercover slimeballs."

"What have you done?"

"You know one of the remaining senators who are also my bodyguard for this place said the two weaklings thought they would have more of a fight left in them."

"WHAT HAVE YOU DONE!"

"You don't know… Han!"

Then a big, six-foot-tall man came up, with a bag that smelled like dead bodies. Sarah looked closer and, to her horror, recognized it as the bodies of Louis Jackson and Jose Mendez, all torn apart.

Sarah went on her knees, in pain, while Smith was delighted by her suffering. They then heard sounds coming from outside the statehouse. Both Smith and this "Han" fellow ran to the other door to escape. McNally saw them escaping and shot Han in the shoulder. Only Smith escaped. McNally grabbed him while rebel forces barged in the statehouse, looking for Smith, but she was already gone. Sarah was still on her knees, feeling somewhat guilty of what happened to both men and what was going to happen to their families.

Chapter 7

JAMES TRUMAN

James Truman. That's me at the scene. When I was "ordered" to escort both Sarah and McNally to the hospital, I asked Sarah what happened.

Sarah said, "What do you think happened?"

Sarah spotted Han with his injured shoulder next to an ambulance. Sarah started yelling for others to nab him. One of the rebels helped him into the ambulance. Sarah was furious. She tried to attack him. I grabbed her and told her to stop.

"Let go of me!" Sarah screamed.

I restrained her and told her to stop because he was surrendering. Sarah explained that this was none of my business.

They drove Han to the emergency room.

Sarah yelled, "No!" and she had a pistol and shot Han in the head through the glass wall. I was shocked, but not nearly as shocked when Talbot came out of nowhere and asked me what I was doing.

"You're disobeying orders."

I explained, "One of your rebels shot an unarmed man."

Then Talbot answered, "You violated my authority!" Talbot threatened to detain me.

I punched him in the cheek and asked, "Really? Well, now you have a real reason to detain me!"

Talbots said, "You're out of line, Truman!"

I answered, "No, you are!"

Talbot then threw me right on the spot. I handed over my weapon to him and left. You know I always wanted to be a hero when I was a kid, so I decided to be a rebel. Naturally, I felt like I wanted to not just punch Talbot but I was so angry I could have killed him. But I always remembered my mother saying, "Getting mad won't help."

Ten years earlier

I was with my lover at the time. We had a rocky relationship. Her name was Celia Mendoza. I met her while she was living in an abusive lifestyle with her family until me and my family raised her. I remember, three weeks later, after we had Celia, my mom was mysteriously murdered. We found out that she was poisoned, but to me, it was no mystery how she died; it was either someone she or her family knew. I'd become very angry with people around me. I felt I just couldn't go through with society, knowing that I lost my mother. I was a lot closer to my mother than my father. My father was a club fighter, the type of place where people smoked, drank, and sometimes used drugs. I heard those people were sometimes business people that my dad had gotten involved with. My dad wasn't good at boxing; in fact, he always lost when he fought. It was the same at home. He got into fights with my mom and always lost in the end.

My dad became an alcoholic after Mom died. It was just me, Dad, and my sister, Karla. We were more like parents than children for my dad. He had lost a great deal when my mom died. We comforted him, with a lot of compassion. Celia would cry if we even mention her because she was like a surrogate parent to her. My dad went to see a shrink, who was my mom's twin brother, Uncle Walter. My uncle tried to help him move on with his life. Sometimes he got misty because Walter looked just like my mom. But it wasn't only that she died but died from a mysterious brain swelling that killed her.

Five years later, I began to tell Celia how I really felt about her and that I'd been wearing a mask half my life, acting all happy, all normal, all nice, but nothing really feels that way. Celia understood and gave me a sad kiss. Two years later, my anger started to grow.

I'd become angrier slowly on the outside. Celia didn't like that I was getting out of control. She secretly began to see my best friend, Kyle Jadiel. I found out that Celia seduced Kyle and lied to him that I broke up with her. I ran into Kyle at the college center and saw Celia and Kyle kissing. I grabbed Kyle and beat him down to the floor. Celia tried to stop me from hitting him. While she was doing so, I blindly smacked her in the face during the fight. I was horrified with the realization that my anger couldn't be kept in check.

I went home and told my father what happened. I told him I needed to disappear. He refused, so I did the most painful thing to say.

I blamed him in front of my sister, who was caught in the middle, saying, "It's your fault Mom is dead!"

Dad screamed, "You can get the hell out of my house for all I care!" Karla tried to stop me, but my dad was holding her, saying, "No point, honey. He's too dead to us."

I could hear Karla screaming when I was leaving. During the first ten years, I'd been starved, was attacked, raped, and left for dead. But I'd managed to survive, study, and even had jobs. One of them was being a rebel. But because I lacked the skills and the talent, I stayed low rank. You might say I was running from my past, and perhaps I was. It had been ten years, and I was thirty years old.

While living in Smart City, I saw someone that looked somewhat familiar to me from my past. I couldn't see well because she was farther away from me.

But when I got the chance to get a good look on her face, I then said to myself, "Celia?" Then I walked even closer, saying, "Hello, miss."

She then said, "Hello." She seemed to not recognize me. I asked her if she needed any help. She answered with a sweet voice, "No, thank you."

"Okay…" Then I saw her walking away, and I knew if I said nothing, I'd lose her forever.

"Celia!"

She stood there in shock until she began to realize who she was speaking to. She looked at me again and became very emotional, with tears all over her face while standing there. She ran off. While she was running, I began to chase her.

"Celia, please don't go!"

We ran for about twenty seconds until she tripped and fell.

I went over and bent my knees to check on her. "Are you okay?"

She started punching me in the chest, yelling, "Don't touch me!"

"Celia, it's me, James."

"I know who you are, lamebrain. It's been five years, and I was doing much better without you."

I looked at her, shocked and sad, saying, "I'm so sorry."

"Well, you should be. After all, I'm talking to a dead man."

I looked at her, confused, and thought to myself, *What does she mean?*

"Why did you even bother, James, after all the grief you just caused?"

I knew I had to say something even though I knew I didn't have a good answer for bringing her so much pain, but I loved her enough to be with her again and to be honest with her. "I…um…"

"What?"

"I missed you."

Celia then laughed at me, saying, "So you decided to come back because you missed me. What if I told you how many times Kyle and your family missed you all combined!"

"Celia… I…"

"Get out of my face!"

I thought to myself that there was no way I could go back after that. I then left her there, and I heard her crying, but I left her because I knew me being with her was good for me.

Then at midnight, on my bed, while thinking of Celia, I could hear loud knocks on the door. I grabbed my pistol in case something happened and opened the door.

I said, "Who's there?"

I was ready to shoot when I realized the person who was knocking was Celia. She told me she wanted to see me.

I said, "Well, come on in."

We talked and drank a couple of beers.

She said, "James, I'm sorry for what happened." I explained to her that it was no problem, but she persisted, saying, "Yes, it is."

"James, I was wrong to treat you like that. It's just, I was so caught up in what happened to me I never stopped and wondered what happened to you. And I should have never cheated on you with John."

I smiled and said, "Celia, I forgive you. But it wasn't just that."

"Then what was it?"

I explained to her the reason I left wasn't that she cheated on me; it was because of the pain of losing my mother and having the stress the take care of my family. I was so angry back then with what happened to my mom that I later thought I had it under control, but I was flipping out many times because I never faced it well.

"But we can help you back home, James."

"I'd love to go home, Celia."

"But what's stopping you?"

"I've almost killed my best friend and smacked you. I insulted my father by blaming him for my mother's death, and I still believe that."

"But that was a long time ago."

"But what happened after that wasn't so long ago."

Then I told her about what I'd been doing for five years. There was a psychologist in Canada I once went to. I even tried yoga to help me find peace of mind, but it didn't last. I had a job as an archeologist in Mexico, and the person I worked with was a former priest. Celia began to cry while I was telling my story and felt so sad or so guilty for what happened to me. I told her that if she wanted to be with me to stay in Smart City. It took her some time to think about it. But then she concluded that she was a grown lady, and if things got bad back in Texas, she decided, so be it.

She decided to stay with me. While she was with me, I met some interesting people along the way, such as John Clay, Jose Mendez, Louis Jackson, Wilfred McNally, and Sarah Barton, just to name a few.

Chapter 8

The Aftermath

The day of both Jackson's and Mendez's funerals was one of the worst times for Sarah. Everyone in the funeral had said that they didn't deserve that kind of death. His death would be a setback in the investigation of Smith. No one would ever know how Jackson and Mendez felt in the presence of Linda Smith and the State. We might not even know if he found more information while facing death.

I could recall, one time, Jackson's ex-wife and Mendez's brother attended to pay their respects all the way from home.

Sarah saw and knew them and said to them, "I'm very sorry."

Then the priest began to bless the bodies of both two rebels. Everybody bowed, and they felt awful and sad.

While everyone was at the funeral, Celia and I were at home, and it had been a week since I hadn't been on the resistance. I didn't want to tell her right away because I felt it would be too embarrassing for me and for her. Then she asked.

"You're okay, sugar?" asked Celia.

"Yeah, babe, I'm all right…"

"Then why do you look kind of gloomy?"

"Ah, it's nothing. Maybe it's this stupid fog that keeps happening in the city."

"Sugar?"

"Babe?"

"Did something happen to you at work?"

At that moment when she asked, "Did something happen to you at work?" I got nervous, and I didn't want to tell her I was suspended. But even if I did lie, she'd still get suspicious anyway. Trust me, I had a lot to deal with after I was suspended. I just wanted to lie down and rest. But before I could either answer Celia's question or even take a day's rest, the phone rang. Celia said it was for me.

It was Talbot. I picked up the phone and said hello.

This conservation on the phone went something like this:

"Yeah, Talbot? So…what…me…no… I can't do that! Look, I'd rather be invisible than do that. You can throw me out for all I care. Oh, wait, you already did!" I slammed the phone down and said under my breath, "Jackass. Must be drunk or something!"

Celia said to me, "You've been thrown out?"

Then I face-palmed.

Celia was furious. But she managed to keep a calm attitude outside. She suggested that we talk about this tomorrow and that I'd accept whatever Talbot wanted me to do and to have me sleep so she could take a breather. But for some reason, I couldn't sleep, so I went and got a beer. I sat in the chair, thinking. I began to feel tired. I went to bed while Celia was outside. I turned off the lights. I sat down on my wooden bed and slumped over the pillow. Then I began to dream.

I was dreaming the same dream I'd been having for the past ten years.

But it wasn't only a dream. It was a nightmare. I saw a series of images of a dead woman next to a green demonic face that looked like human skin. My body couldn't move. I feared that I might have been sleep paralyzed. I heard a voice that sounded like my father, over and over, while this was happening, "James! James! James!" and everything became red, like blood on my face.

I woke up at 10:58 p.m., and I felt as if lightning shocked me. I saw Celia asleep with me, and I felt isolated. I realized how much I missed my family, but the one person I didn't miss was my father.

And I said, "I want to go home…but I don't want to know about mental help."

A few minutes later, I decided to call on the phone, but I decided not to call for my family but for Talbot, to accept his offer to replace either Mendez or Jackson. The next day, I wasn't in the mood to say anything after that godforsaken nightmare. I realized I was late for work. The alarm clock read 10:44 a.m., which meant I was late. I hurried up and put my jumpsuit on so I could be identified. I had to skip breakfast and shower because I was so late. Celia was annoyed that I was making so much noise. She asked me what was wrong. I told her I was late.

I grabbed my pistol, and she said, "Late for what? You're out of the resistance."

"That was before I accepted Talbot's offer."

She saw how I was acting and was a bit concerned for me. I told her I was fine, but each time she asked, she started to annoy me also.

She said to me, "Look, you seem upset. What's wrong?"

"Not now, Celia."

I told her to stop asking me what was wrong. I told her it was not the right time. But she persisted.

"Yes, it is, James, because I'm your girlfriend."

At that moment, she was starting to get on my nerves. I spelled it out right in front of her.

"Uh, whatever… I'm sorry." At that moment, I felt like a total jerk. I totally chewed on the one person from my past who was by my side, who had never given up on me, and I basically said whatever.

She looked at me, surprised, and said, "It's 11:04. You better get going."

"Celia… I—"

"Don't!"

Then, with a sad look on my face, I jumped into my car and started driving to work.

Chapter 8

The Attack on the Resistance

As I was driving, I saw the area where the rebels were going. When I went in, I saw a lot of people talking in groups. As I got closer, I could see that they were angry. Even Sarah was angry. The only one who wasn't was Talbot.

He greeted me by saying, "Oh, Jimmy boy, nice to see you accepting your promotion. Now, according to your records, you should be like Mendez, right?"

"I..."

"Perfect!"

Everyone in the room gave me a dirty look. Talbot took me into a room where I was going to be in. I saw a name plaque that read "Mendez." Talbot saw that I was looking at the plaque, and he turned and ripped it off. I knew in that moment that Talbot was just trying to cause trouble. Every single rebel looked at both me and Talbot. When I walked into the room, it looked and smelled horrible. After I was inside, I tried to work through it despite having the awful odor around me. I check on the internet to see any updates on what was going on in the city. Then, about ten minutes later, while searching, I felt a sting on my neck. I touched to see what it was, then I realized it was a tranquilizer dart, and I fell to the floor, unconscious.

After I was knocked out, about ten to fifteen minutes later, I heard shots fired outside my office. I rushed out and wasn't surprised to find out who hit me in the head. It was Linda Smith and her thugs, wanting payback at Sarah, McNally, and Talbot for deceiving them as senators.

Smith yelled, "I'm looking for three stooges named McNally, Barton, and Talbot."

The other rebels were forced to be removed; if not, Smith would have killed them and their family. Not a single one of them even put up a fight to defend our team. The senators identified the three officers and brought them to her face-to-face. I was absolutely shocked and disgusted by how cowardly the department had become.

I was in the corner, watching the whole thing happen, with my pistol next to me. Smith then split the three rebels in different areas. Nobody noticed me for a while until I accidently made a crack sound with my foot on the floor, and Barton saw my shoulder but didn't recognize me at all, but did think I was crazy.

However, Smith didn't notice me hiding but did see a look on Sarah's face and asked, "What the hell is your problem?"

Sarah replied, "You!"

Smith pointed a gun at her and said, "Say what, bitch!"

She was ready to shoot her when suddenly I jumped, with my pistol pointing at Smith, saying what Sarah said, "You!"

Then I shot Smith in the arm. Sarah then punched her in the mouth, and it seemed like we then got her. But then her senators jumped in and shot me in the heel and fell to the floor. I remembered the pain I felt and the type of voice I screamed while I was shot. I wasn't able to help Sarah when Smith then smacked her in the face and was ready to shoot her until McNally and Talbot decided to grow some balls and jumped on Smith. The senators held McNally and Talbot.

Smith got up and was ready to shoot both in the chest, but then Sarah shot Smith in the ribs and was bleeding so much Smith said to the two senators while spitting blood, "Next time, boys. Let's get out of here."

McNally and Talbot were pushed to the floor. Both tried to run after them. Talbot ordered McNally to take the left side, and Talbot would take the right side. McNally ran to see if anyone was there. He saw a senator walking by.

McNally yelled, "Hold it!"

The senator tried to run. McNally chased after the guy, but then the guy started spraying bullets with an Uzi. Then McNally pulled out his pistol and shot the senator in the back of the leg. The senator started saying a lot of crap against McNally. McNally would have none of it. He then cuffed the bastard and was ready to go to the department, waiting for Talbot to be finished.

Out of mercy, McNally patched the senator's wounds, and the senator said, "Why're you doing this? You know who I am."

McNally explained, "I know what you are, but I don't know who you are."

A few minutes later, while patching up both me and Sarah, we all got worried and believed something was wrong. Then a phone rang, with Talbot's number.

Sarah then picked it up, saying, "Yeah, boss."

"If you want Talbot to live, you better do something for me."

"Go to hell, Smith!" She was ready to hang up until she heard a scream that was from Talbot getting electrocuted.

Sarah was horrified, and Smith spoke again, saying, "Come again?"

"Okay, just tell me what you want me to do."

"First, shut up and listen!"

"Okay! Okay!"

"Good, here's what you're going to do."

When the phone call was over, I asked Sarah what was wrong, and she said to me what they did to Talbot. I was forced to let all of us go and take Talbot back, but she insisted that we do what they say to make that happen.

I asked her, "Then what do they want in exchange?"

"Flakka."

"What?"

"I know, but we don't have any choice."

This new mission that Sarah now temporarily took to save Talbot's life seemed like all hope was lost, hope for a better future not just for Smart City but the whole world. But like I said, believing when you had a choice was one thing, but another when you really didn't have a choice.

Chapter 9

Saving Mark Talbot

I felt so guilty about what happened to Talbot, and the guilt got worse when all of us were puzzled and wondered what we were going to do now.

We continued to freak out, with no idea, and said to each other, "Even if we trade with her, she will still kill us."

"How do you know that?" I said.

"Because she is a mentally ill psychopath."

While all of us were panicking, we heard a loud voice that almost bled our ears.

"Hold it!"

All of us covered our ears and thought to ourselves, *What the hell was that?*

It turned out it was Sarah, who told all of us straight to our faces, "Are you rebels or cowards?"

We were shocked and thought to ourselves, *Who does she think she is?* But slowly we began to understand that maybe she was right, and we had been acting like a bunch of cowards.

"If any of you want to cry or give up, you might as well take away your pistol and get out!"

We looked at each other, saying, "What if she's right?"

Then I heard a rebel yell out while removing his pistol, "I don't care if she's right. I won't help. I have a family to take care of, and I plan not to let them see me dead because of a trade gone bad."

I told the rebel next to me, "You're a rebel."

"Not anymore."

Then I saw a group of five then twelve rebels, and almost all cops quit their jobs. I couldn't believe what I just saw, but I bet not as much as Sarah and McNally, who were the only two rebels left besides me.

Sarah then looked at me, saying, "Are you going to leave too?"

I smiled at her and said, "Never."

"So what are we going to do about the senator?" Sarah said.

Then McNally approached the senator that he showed mercy toward and said, "You want to get off here?"

Then the senator looked at McNally, saying, "More than anything."

"Help us stop Smith, and we'll get you out here."

Then the guy started shaking and trembling as if he was conflicted to make that type of choice. So instead of answering, he just stood there, shivering.

"You're okay?" McNally said.

Then the guy went up and grabbed his pistol. We all were ready to shoot him, but McNally told us to put our guns down. He tried to reason with him, saying, "Killing yourself isn't a smart move, kid."

But the guy just couldn't take it. He yelled out, "I don't care!"

He then shot himself in the head, and blood came on McNally's face.

We were in total shock, but not as shocked as McNally. He then said, "May God have mercy on him!"

About two hours later, Sarah McNally and I decided to go at nighttime so that the senators wouldn't see us so good. Then the three of us drove in separate vehicles, one with a pistol, the other with a knife, and the last one with a sniper rifle. So the three of us went in, except McNally, who was helping us take down the guards and kill the lights; besides, he had enough stress as it was.

We could get inside the statehouse without any problems. Sarah explained how she knew every area inside while undercover. I followed her to the basement, where she believed Talbot was, just like Mendez was. We went down and heard a muffling sound as if a person was gagged from the mouth. We went down, believing it was Talbot, but to our horror and shock, we realized it was the sound of a woman, all tied up and beaten.

"Jesus Christ," I said.

Sarah and I went to help her down, and we did.

Sarah said to the gal, "Are you okay?"

Then she was crying and hugging Sarah. Sarah hesitated, but she went and embraced her. That was the first time I saw Sarah's softer side. Until it turned out that the gal started to laugh, and Sarah recognized that laugh, which made her paralyzed with fear. The laughing came from Linda Smith in disguise.

"You're all going to die!" she said.

After speaking, both me and Sarah were grabbed from the back by two bulky and ugly senators. Me and Sarah were sent outside to be killed.

Sarah yelled out to Smith, "Where is Talbot?"

Smith said, "In a place to keep an eye on."

"You know one of us has a sniper ready to take you out," I said.

"You mean this sniper?"

Me and Sarah saw McNally, all bruised and bloody and held by another one of those creeps. Sarah became so enraged I saw her face looking red like blood.

"I'll kill you!"

"In your dreams, you red-haired bimbo!"

Sarah struggled with one of the senators to get out, taking down Smith once and for all.

Smith began to laugh then said to Sarah, "Ha, what are you doing now, bitch!"

While Smith was laughing over and over, both us thought that this was the end, so much so our own faces, according to McNally, looked like we lost all hope. But at the same time, we made ourselves appear somehow, in a strange way, strong. Yet it was obvious that we were afraid. But before they were ready to make their move, somebody out of nowhere knocked out Smith in the head with a pistol and shot the three senators in the head. Turned out, it was Mark Talbot, the chief of police. It seemed that McNally found Talbot first and allowed himself to get captured for Talbot to save us and capture Smith.

"Did you miss me?" said Talbot.

"But, Chief, how did you escape?"

"It was McNally."

Talbot explained that McNally found him and allowed him to get captured for Talbot to save him with the help of a paper clip.

"You gotta be kidding me."

"Does it look like I'm joking, Truman?"

One day later, Talbot and all of us decided to do a war against the State; but before we did so, we took Smith into our department, and afterward, we could convince about two to eight resigned rebels to come back to the resistance. We then got ourselves in a negotiation with the State to bring Smith back and they would treat us better. We thought this was a good idea, but Talbot basically said to them, "Go to hell!" So this started a revolution, and an extreme bloodbath came to the streets of Smart City. Almost all of us, including McNally, were severely injured and thought we were going to lose. Because of the State's advanced technology, I knew that we had to do this. But sometimes I wondered if it was worth it even though I believed that it was now. It seemed crazy.

While all of this was happening, a senator came a few blocks away and was about to shoot Talbot and Sarah, who were carrying McNally and a few other injured rebels to safety in a corner.

I yelled out, "Hey, scumbag!" I then took aim and shot the wacko in the face when he turned to me.

While blood filled the streets and hope seemed to be lost, I saw civilians with trash cans and other garbage, like metal or glass, being thrown at the senators. Then both Sarah and I were told to bring the injured cops to safety while Talbot was ready to blow the statehouse to hell.

We were about to leave until I saw a couple of civilians shot at. One was a woman, the other a child by the senators. I became horrified and angry, especially when the shooters laughed at the victims. I then went and shot the shooters in the stomach and in the pelvis.

Sarah looked at me and said, "What are you doing?"

I said to her what she said to all of us when she planned to help Talbot. "Am I a rebel or a coward?"

I then rescued the two injured civilians. But then I saw an old man on the floor, so I rushed to bring the first two to safety and brought the old fellow to safety also while shooting the senators. After all that, we rushed to the hospital. We knew that the hospital wouldn't have as great doctors as they did before World War III. But I knew we had no choice. Sarah called the ambulance. While calling the phone, a huge explosion came from the statehouse. We jumped in shock, wondering, *What was that?* Then after the explosion, we then saw a huge tank with the State symbol. And we thought, What *is going on?' Didn't we win?*

The tank just stood there for about three minutes. Both rebels and senators were afraid and wondered who was inside. But then the senators smiled and were cheering, and we closed our eyes, with our heads down. But then, while they were cheering, they got blown to bits. And we became shocked and realized that it wasn't a senator inside there; it was one of our own. It was Mark Talbot.

He then went out of the tank and said, "Hey, Truman, remind me to get you a better office."

Then we smiled, cheered, and laughed. It was not only us but also civilians too, who felt they regained their freedom. We all, for the first time in years, felt like we regained our freedom.

Chapter 10

Meet the Bartons

After the state war was over, Smith was sent to Life's Garden Hospital for the criminally insane. To me, I felt she needed someplace worse. But because of Smith's fascist laws that we were still trying to fix, no one could get a trial. But after all the hell we had been through, Talbot told all of us to take the day off. So then I did what they asked and went home. Back home, I remembered laying down on the bed, waiting to tell my fiancée, Celia, what happened. But I found out she was still working in her job as a bartender. With my whole body there, I felt exhausted and went to sleep.

Four hours later, I had a phone call from Sarah, who wanted me to go visit both her and Dr. Barton. I explained to her, my fiancée wasn't home yet, but I would visit when she came back. Then I went back to sleep.

Then, in about twelve minutes, I heard the door being knocked, and I realized it was Celia outside. I began to yawn and got myself out of bed. I opened the door, and she still had a grudge over what happened this morning.

"Celia, I—"

"If you are going to say sorry, James, it's too late."

"Don't tell me you're still having a grudge over that."

Celia got mad and yelled at me, "Of course, I'm still having a grudge over that!"

I decided to calm down and went up to her and said, "No, you're right. I was a jerk in that moment. You have every right to mad, Celia."

"Sometimes I wondered why I'd throw my life to come to yours."

"And sometimes I wonder if I should come back home."

Celia looked at me and touched me in the cheek, saying, "The reason you left home is because of you and your father."

"Sometimes I wished he was a better person."

"You can't change other people, James. You can only change yourself. Want to relax, James?"

"Yes…um, no."

"Why?"

"I got news for you."

I explained to her that we beat the State, and she thought I was joking until she realized I wasn't joking and said, "Are you crazy?"

She checked to see if there was any injury in my body until she went up to my face, and we sort of blushed. Until I remembered the special visit I was offered by the Bartons. I explained it to Celia, and she was very interested. We decided to go meet each other in our civilian jumpsuits and drove all the way to a place that looked like the house from the opening scene of the movie *Halloween*, yet ours looked like the inside of a hotel, so who was I to judge?

We went in, and I heard Celia say to me, "James?"

I said to her, "Yeah, Celia."

"How do I look?"

I smiled and told her that she looked nice as always. I told her that they might have brought some beer in the house, and I didn't want her to be disturbed to think I would go crazy with it. She explained to me that beer was beer, so what was the difference?

I answered her by saying, "The flavor." I then chuckled a bit because of the way I said it.

I realized my boots were untied. I told her it would take a few seconds. But then instantly I heard the door open, and my heart started to freeze. I looked up and saw both Sarah and Patrick Barton in front of me, with a friendly smile.

Sarah looked and said to me, "Hello, Truman."

I was a bit embarrassed to meet them while tying my boots, but they never held a grudge over me. I shook both Sarah's and Patrick's hands.

"Hello, Sarah…and this is?"

The man who I questioned was a bit confused, looking for about two seconds until Sarah nudged him, and he said, "Oh. I'm her husband. My name is Patrick."

I shook his hand again, saying, "Sorry about that."

"No worries."

Then Sarah looked at Celia and said to me, "Who's this?"

I smiled, saying, "She's my fiancée. Her name is Celia."

Celia also shook Sarah's hand and said, "Nice to see you."

Sarah said, "Likewise."

Then we decided to go inside the house and meet each other. When we went inside, I had a feeling as if there was something more to this than what Sarah was telling me. At the same time, I decided to just go along with this, only to know what was really going on.

When we were inside, we all talked and had a very comfortable time, without violence, without worries, and without pain. It was like something out of a dream. I remembered something that Sarah told me while we were eating on the table, a lot of things that made me laugh around with Celia and Patrick.

One of the things she said was, "You should be the next leader of the resistance."

I laughed, saying, "Yeah, fat chance."

"No, I'm serious about kicking Smith's ass. That was fantastic!"

"You did some good of your own."

"But who went first?" It was like a wonderful moment; even in a dark world with no tomorrow, at least some joy still existed. Then Sarah looked at me and asked me a serious question. "Truman?"

I answered, "Yeah?"

"Would you like to be my partner on the force?"

I replied, "I already have one."

Sarah said, "Who?"

"My fiancée." Both I and Celia chuckled a little.

"No, Truman, I mean seriously."

I then realized she was really serious, and I said to her, "No, I don't."

I asked her why she wanted to know. Sarah explained, because if we were going to get Talbot, she needed someone with good aim.

I told her I was lucky and that I was also a trainee.

"Maybe you're right. But what I saw is someone who deserves more than being called a trainee."

I then smiled at her. A few seconds later, we all chuckled for a bit. Until I began to break down with tears in my eyes.

Celia looked at me, saying, "James, what's wrong, honey…"

"I'm sorry. I'm so sorry."

I got up and then decided to take some fresh air.

Celia looked at both Dr. Barton and Sarah and said, "I'm sorry. He's never been like this before… We'll be back."

Then Sarah looked at us with compassion and said, "It's okay. If there's anything wrong, we understand."

One of the things I recalled was being on the bench and having a feeling as if my heart was broken. I felt Celia's palm on my shoulder, and I felt like an embarrassment to her…and she was also much more embarrassed than me but at the same time was compassionate enough because she looked into my eyes and knew what I was remembering—something bad a long time ago.

I started to tremble and ran outside.

Celia looked at Dr. Barton and Sarah and said, "I'm so sorry…" Then she followed me outside to the bench. I had a cigarette on my mouth when Celia asked me what happened.

I replied, "I don't want to talk about it."

"You want to go home?" Celia said.

"No," I said.

"Want to stay for a bit?"

"No."

"Then what?"

"Look, Celia!"

Then Celia yelled out and said, "Don't you 'Look, Celia' me! You're acting like a five-year-old who just broke his ankle and is really starting to get on my nerves. Now tell me what's wrong!"

I started to give her the silent treatment for a few seconds until I said, "Memories…"

"What?"

I looked at her with both my eyes, without saying anything. Then she understood what I was thinking about.

She then replied, "James, I'm so sorry."

Then I felt bad and sympathetic that I argued with her, and now she was feeling pity for me because I told her how I felt.

I then touched her on the cheek very softly and said, "No, babe. I'm the one who should be sorry."

I also explained to her that I would be nice if things would be back to normal.

Then we looked at the streets and couldn't believe that the world wanted to destroy itself, and for what? Earth was indeed a utopia, but seeing it now with my lover, all I could say was, *Which is better, to live life as a slave or to die free as a soldier?*

After I was finished talking with Celia, we decided to take only a few minutes with Sarah and Patrick and leave. We took some time inside the house. They wondered if anything was wrong. We told them everything was fine. We smiled and chuckled, and I even had an arm-wrestling contest with me and Sarah to see who would win. I felt embarrassed in the end to lose to a girl, but I denied the theory that I lost because I was scrawny. So then me and Celia said our goodbyes, and for the first time, while leaving the house, we felt a sense of peace that both of us hadn't had in years.

When we went home, both of us just fell to the floor with our clothes on. We laughed and laughed for quite a while because, for the first time in this godforsaken world, we were happy. Then tears came to our eyes while we looked at each other. And then for about a few minutes, we had gone to sleep.

I had this dream of Celia and I walking to go inside our car. But then I saw men and women that looked extremely furious at us, and they began to run toward us. We rushed to the car, but then I saw the men and women grab Celia before I could even open the car. Then I saw them body-slamming her to the floor and were laughing and calling toilet names at her. I was about to jump on those bastards when suddenly I was shot by one of them on the knee. Another held my head to watch Celia being raped by them. I struggled to take their hands off me, but they were far too strong. I was bleeding and crying over and over. But when one of them who I recognized as Linda Smith came up and aimed a Magnum gun at her, I saw Celia's face, looking helpless and scared. She then closed her eyes and was killed.

After they fired at her, I woke, back home, in pure sweat. I saw Celia on the left side of our bed.

She saw me with a terrified expression on my face and said, "James, what's wrong?"

My eyes turned to her, and I felt myself slowly able to breathe again, knowing that she was still alive. I then smiled and said, "Oh, nothing, just a false alarm."

Then she looked at me and said with a very soft voice, "If there is anything wrong, you can tell me, James."

"It's okay, babe I just had…" At that moment, I didn't know what to say because I was filled with a lot of emotions at that moment.

She then asked me, "Was it another nightmare?"

"Yeah."

Then I laid my head on her legs, and she asked me what it was about. I then explained to her that I saw Smith and the senators kill her.

Celia looked at me and said, "That's terrible."

"I know…"

Then she put my chin up and said to me directly, "I'm not leaving you, James."

Then she kissed me. And we both went back to sleep.

While I was sleeping, I remembered a lot of things from my youth. But one of the things that stuck to my head for years was, after my mother, it was thanksgiving, and my dad was sent to this rage. Me and my sister tried to calm him down. One time he slapped us and warned us in a loud voice, "Don't make me kill you."

He then left us alone in the house and came back drunk from the bar. I and Karla went up to help, and Karla understood even at a young age that our own father was becoming dark. I remembered, after that, I knew my life would never be the same.

I then woke up. I began to wonder if these dreams or memories would ever stop. Or did I really want them to stop?

Chapter 11

LINDA SMITH COMMITTED!

After I woke up, I drove down to the resistance. I parked my car and walked inside. I saw all the rebels there again like it was back to normal, and it seemed less corrupt than it was before. Then I saw Sarah and McNally walking toward me.

One of them said, "Good to see you, James."

But when I was about to thank them, I had a strange feeling out of nowhere that something bad was going to happen.

I stopped talking for about a few seconds until Sarah looked at me, saying, "Are you okay?"

"Yeah. Just nothing."

I thought I was just being paranoid and nothing serious, and I shrugged it off and forgot about it. Then the three of us decided to go meet the chief again. But nobody was there, except a piece of paper, saying, "I'll be back in five minutes." So the three of us began to talk and get to know each other more. I remember telling McNally about how many people I fought in the streets before I became a rebel.

He told me, "Well, aren't you a badass."

"Aw, you're making me blush."

"Like roses, Rosie."

"Man, screw you!"

McNally and Sarah laughed, and so did I, a little.

McNally then said afterward, "But in all seriousness, good job, James."

I smiled and looked around and said, "By the way, how long will Talbot come?"

Then a voice that sound like Robert de Niro came out of nowhere and said to me in a high voice, "I'm here."

All of us began to feel a bit curious after everything that just happened. Even more curious was when we beat the State.

Talbot said to us, "Rebels, I know we are having a great day in rebuilding, and what's greater is that other states and countries are doing the same."

We began to smile and believed that was it, and we would live in a world without tyranny and dictatorship. Then we thought to ourselves, *What else?* He then explained that even though the state-house and senators were gone, one problem remained. Was Linda Smith truly insane, or was she just faking it to regain power both in the hospital and everything?

Sarah told the chief, "Chief, we are already having enough of this psychopath, and besides, we won."

"Or did we?"

"What do you mean?" I said.

"Smith is very smart, maybe smarter. She is perhaps one of the evilest women in the face of history. Did you know, while she was a politician, she manipulated her own world by saying she was a woman of peace?"

McNally then said, "And this connects her to Life's Garden because?"

"What I'm trying to say is, if she can trick the whole world, imagine what she can do in a mental hospital from Smart City."

We all thought that Talbot had a point and were worried even more for what was to come.

Sarah then asked, "What are you suggesting?"

"Go to Life's Garden and tell the doctors that you wish to see her."

"You mean interrogate her," said McNally.

"Whatever. It sounds better when I say it."

So the three of us had a new mission and was to go to Life's Garden Hospital and have a little chat with the doctors to have a little chat with Linda Smith herself.

We then drove for about thirty-five minutes. We had a plan to let Sarah stay in the car, with a sniper this time, while me and McNally would go inside with walkie-talkies in case we needed to back up.

We went to the hospital, asking someone who worked in the hospital, saying, "Me and my friend would like to speak with the patient."

The person who was asking was named Nabeel Toameh, director of Life's Garden Hospital. He asked us, "Are you a relative?"

"No," we told him.

"You have to be a relative or a friend to go visit the patient."

"Sir, I insist you let us go see inside."

"I'm sorry, I can't do that," Toameh said.

Out of nowhere, we saw him twitching, and both of us looked at each other in suspicion.

I was a little bit creeped out, but McNally didn't really care and went up to Toameh, saying in a streaky voice, "Look, we are part of the resistance."

"I understand that, but this is private property. Nobody can enter, not unless you two have a legal reason from the State."

"Sir, don't you know that the State is finished," I said.

"In here, gentlemen, nothing's finished." And he started to slightly grin while he was finishing.

I whispered to McNally, "The guy is pretty creepy."

While I was saying this, McNally had a plan that shocked both me and Toameh by bribing him with an old, crummy-looking hundred-dollar bill that McNally had before the third war.

"What the hell are you doing?" I said.

"What does it look like I'm doing?"

Toameh was standing there in shock and might have thought to himself, *How can he bribe me?* I thought he was going to call security until, to my surprise, he accepted the money.

Toameh said, "Dumb move for a dumb blond. Get out of here before I call security!"

"What about 150… Well?" said McNally.

Then Toameh decided to give in. McNally said, "See, was that so hard?"

"Don't think this will happen again, blondie!"

Finally, Toameh allowed us to go upstairs and talk to Smith to see if everything was really in order. While we went upstairs, both me and McNally were talking about the mission.

I asked him "Do you want me to interrogate her?"

"Yeah, sure, why not?"

I asked him again, "Do you want to play good cop / bad cop?"

Then McNally smiled and said, "Sure, but how about you go be a good cop first, and then I'll be a bad cop."

Then we went to a certain room called Room 5. We saw her, and I could remember how much that could still piss off a person. When McNally and I were inside her room, her head was down, and she acted like we weren't there. The two of us looked at each other like, *What the hell is this?*

But he shrugged it off and went forward with the mission.

"Want to try, James?"

"Sure." I decided to approach her, but nothing seemed to happen. So then I began to talk to her. "Okay, Smith."

She was just standing there like a statue and not saying a word. Then I explained to her all her victims that she killed from the past that led her to this point.

"You see, Smith, you see, after all the deaths and innocent people you killed, nobody is going to help you this time. Not your father. Not your old pals from D. C. Not even the State itself can help you anymore because, apparently, they're all gone."

And she kept refusing to speak and kept pretending to be an empty vessel.

"Fine, don't talk, but you are not helping yourself. Instead, you're screwing with someone who you don't want to screw with!"

Then McNally came out of nowhere and yelled out, "All right, this is getting boring!" And then he shrugged me by the shoulder and said, "Stand aside, Truman!"

He then grabbed Smith by the shirt, and I said, "McNally! McNally!"

"What?"

"Look!"

Then we saw Smith's eyes looking like someone who just had a huge dose of Flakka.

Both us then said, "Oh god!" And then we ran out and closed the door outside the room. Smith came up, banging it over and over.

McNally looked at me while both of us were holding the door, saying, "How did she get drugged?"

"Maybe a mole came in and injected her!" I said.

"But who?"

"Right now, McNally, I don't really give a crap. I just want to survive."

"No kidding," McNally said.

While we were holding Smith, there came along Sarah, who was outside the car, now rushing in to defend us.

"Whoa, look at her. She got freaking red eyes. Maybe she's high or…nope, she's high," said McNally.

"Just help us with this please!" Sarah said to McNally.

"Okay, it's not like I or Toameh drugged her or something!"

Then both Sarah and I had an epiphany. Both of us thought, if the director of the hospital didn't know that she was drugged, then we didn't know who else.

I then said to McNally, "What did you say?"

A voice loud enough to be a microphone came and said, "You shouldn't have got involved."

We realized that the voice was indeed Nabeel Toameh.

Sarah looked shocked while holding the door and said, "Nabeel, you're my husband's boss and friend. Why would you do this?"

"Look, Sarah, I didn't want to do this at first, but then I realized there really is no hope forever."

"And working with psychopaths is going to help you?"

"Do you know what happened?" Toameh said.

"What?"

"Wow, you really don't know… Flakka."

"What have you done?" Sarah said.

"What have I done? Smith did it to me, and I did it to her."

"Why would you allow that psycho to touch you!"

And Toameh started to laugh over and over, and then he explained himself, saying, "Because I fell in love."

"You're insane. She doesn't love you. She doesn't love anybody. She only seduced you to get what she wants," Sarah said.

"And what's that!"

"Freedom."

"Oh, like years ago, remember out of all people, you and Patrick trust me the most like family, and enough to keep your secrets. What if I told them in front of you about your past?"

Then Sarah became both shocked and angry, saying, "Shut up!"

"In Mexico."

"Shut up!"

"I know who you are and why you came here."

"I'm serious, Nabeel. Shut up!"

"Oh, Sonya?"

"Chingate cabron!"

Then Sarah gasped, and Toameh laughed. We were very furious as he was laughing at us. Until Sarah came up with an idea for me, and McNally held the door while Sarah tried to find Toameh. I tried to stop her in case Smith started coming out of the door.

While holding it, I heard a voice that yelled, "Help!" but I ignored it until the voice came up again, yelling, "James, get up here!"

Then I realized who it was, but if I let go, Smith would escape. About a few minutes later, I told McNally, "Run!"

He looked at me and said, "What?"

"Run, you clown!"

After both of us stopped ourselves from subduing Smith, we ran off to find Sarah while Smith was God knows where.

The both of us went to the director's office and found Toameh holding Sarah hostage with her gun. While holding the gun, Toameh told us to drop our weapons.

I then tried to come closer to reach him, but he took a shot that was almost close to my foot and said, "Back off!"

"You think you're going to get away with this?" I said.

"Yes, I am, unless you want me to shoot her."

"Dude, you're going to wish you had stayed in Gaza!"

"Yeah, how's that?"

About five seconds of being held hostage, Sarah tried to find a way to escape. She then had an idea to step on Toameh's toe as hard as she could. While doing so, she grabbed the gun and shot Toameh. She went along with it and broke his toe. Sarah was able to retrieve her gun, yet at the same time, Toameh jumped on her after having his foot crushed. McNally and I tried to have Toameh get his filthy hands off Sarah, but the guy was tough, with all that Flakka crap.

While trying to choke her to death, he then yelled out in a very cold and vicious voice, "Touch my girl, and your brain will be charcoaled." That was the day when Sarah knew that Toameh was too far gone.

After about eighteen minutes of violence, we managed to have Toameh off Sarah. Strangely, the guy started laughing.

Sarah then said, "What are laughing at, you freak?"

But he ignored us and kept on laughing. Sarah started to get pretty pissed off and told us to spook him.

McNally held Toameh down to the floor while I put a pistol to his mouth and said, "Look at me, Toameh. Don't make me do this. If you want to be clean, shut up!"

"Oh, I don't think you want me to."

"And why's that?"

Toameh smiled with a dark grin on his face and told us why he was laughing with just one word, "Smith."

"Tell me where she is," I said.

"Go to hell."

"Joke's on you. This is hell, and I'm the devil!"

Then, out of intimidation, I began to choke on him basically until his eyes popped. About three minutes later, he decided he had enough and told us where she was going.

He said, "At your house!"

We all gasped, and he started to laugh. Then Sarah decided to shoot him in the head. Blood spurred out my face to my knees. While kneeling, McNally went back to the car, but Sarah stayed and could tell that I was in shock.

She put her hand on my shoulder and said, "Let him go, James. We got to save your gal." She then felt compassion and tried to find me a towel. When she found it, she gave it to me and said, "Here, wipe it off and get going."

About three seconds later, I wiped some of the blood off my face and went off.

Chapter 12

The Man in Black

Myself, Sarah, and McNally all went to the car and were going out of our minds. I was driving and started to look more and more like some guy who just went insane. I drove so out of control I almost started hitting pedestrians. There was this heart-jumping moment when a kid was walking by, and I probably could have killed him if it weren't for Sarah yelling, "That's enough!" And I turned to her, then she looked at me like she saw the devil. She would later tell me that I turned pale, with red eyes, and my voice sounded like I was snarling.

About two minutes in, we made it to my house. We all went up to open the door, but it was locked. So I rang the doorbell.

When that didn't work, I started to bang the door, yelling, "Celia! Celia!" Then Sarah told McNally to shoot the lock off. While doing so, we got in, then I yelled even harder, "Celia! Celia!"

Next, we were searching around the room to find her, but it was clean, with no sign of struggle or even assault until I stepped on a note, saying, "One down, two to go." While having the note, I started to flip out and went berserk. Sarah and McNally started restraining me, but I was yelling over and over, "First, my mother, then my sister, now her!"

"James. We are going to get them back!" said Sarah.

"You don't know that!"

"Yes. Yes, I do!"

About thirteen seconds of being held on, the three of us started to hear a clicking sound.

Then McNally said, "Is your fire alarm on?"

After about one minute, I saw Sarah's eyes bug out. She threw us outside, yelling, "Get down!"

It turned out that the alarm was really a bomb. After it went off it, it burned the entire house in flames.

"No! No! No!" I yelled.

While seeing my house on fire, I tried to get back in. Sarah pulled my arm back, saying, "James, it's gone!"

"No, shut up. It's not gone!" I said.

"James…"

"Shut up. I'm going to save it!" Then I take off her hand away from my arm so I could run back and try to save it. But then she jumped down and started to hold on to my neck.

She then said to me, "Look at the damn house!" I put my face down. Sarah then said to me, "James, I'm sorry. I'm so sorry. But we have to keep going. Look, I'll drive this time."

Then I went up and tried to walk back to the car when suddenly I saw McNally randomly went down to the floor.

Sarah yelled, "McNally, what's wrong!" then she felt down as well, with a very drowsy look in her eyes.

I then understood what it was when I saw something behind her neck. And I knew it was a tranquilizer dart.

I said to myself, "Oh, terrific!"

About four seconds later, I fell to the floor, but I wasn't knocked out yet; however, my eyes were blurry. While I was still conscious, I saw a man, but he wasn't dressed in green or even in red. He was dressed in black. About two seconds later, I was unconscious.

But it was one second after I woke up, wondering what the hell was going on. Then my eyes were dazed by the bright light that turned out to be a bulb. Suddenly I was slapped in the face, and my senses were clearer, but it still hurt like hell. I looked around and saw both Sarah and McNally, tied up in two chairs next to me. I myself was also tied up.

By the time I looked around, I yelled out, "Sarah! McNally!" but I realized they couldn't hear me. They were beaten too badly. I saw Sarah, all bitten and bloodied, and I saw McNally, all scratched and cut open; then I was slapped again, but this time even harder to the point my nose started bleeding.

I yelled to whoever was slapping me, "Will someone just stop slapping me!"

"But I like to slap people!"

I looked up and saw the same guy dressed in black. He had a fedora hat, with a mask on that covered his whole face.

"And who are you, sock-face?"

"You really don't remember me, do you?"

"Oh yeah, you're the douche who shot us with a tranquilizer dart, and what else, you're going to tell me where our loved ones are."

Then he chuckled and slapped me in the face again, but this time he might have broken my nose.

"I suggest you shut the hell up, boy!"

"Go to hell!"

He was about to slap me again when suddenly I heard a voice yelling at the man in black.

"Enough!"

I realized the voice was none other than Linda Smith. I was horrified and wanted to get the hell of here. I tried to break out from the ropes, but then I heard a chain from underneath the chair that was connected to stay there; to make matters worse, the chain and the ropes were together.

While I was so desperately trying to escape, I also tried to scream for help, but nobody would come. The more I screamed, the more this guy in black and Smith would be amused with me. They were glad that I was screaming for help so much so they started to laugh uncontrollably and made jokes at me, saying, "What are you going to do, scream loud enough for my ears to bleed?"

"No, wait. He probably wants us to give him his bottle."

Then Smith came to me and yelled, "Shut up!" She explained to me that no one was going to help, but she would. Then she called for the man in black to get something from his briefcase that was filled with guns and tranquilizer darts. And lastly… Flakka.

"No!" I said, then Smith ordered the man in black to inject me with the drug. I began to struggle away, but when he got closer, I realized it was pointless. Smith started laughing loudly.

I was almost about to be injected, but I was tossing around while sitting on the chair to the point the man in black slapped me hard enough so I could shut up, and for the first time since I lost my mother, I felt helpless and powerless to do anything.

Smith then came to me and whispered in my ear, "Welcome to an eternity in hell." And she spat on my face.

About a few seconds later, my arm was pulled out without any alcohol or tourniquet I was injected with.

Smith then said, "Tell me, Truman, how many injections it would take? Just one to loosen your screws."

Then they began to laugh over and over and over. During all this, I was remembering my mother, Karla, Celia, and how I might never see them again and how sad it must be for them to see me like this. I was in so much anxiety in pain I wanted to cry, but instead of crying, I was laughing.

My mind was becoming a melting pile of liquid. I was losing every sense of my mind. My skin was just clawing me on the inside. My veins were looking like it was about to pop out, with a lot of blood and crap out. In these moments, I really could feel myself losing a grip by laughing over and over.

While the insanity continued, I began to hear voices and horrific visions even worse than my own nightmares. I found myself going down to a pit. The more it happened, the more I wanted to die.

I began to feel a cut in my skin, and then, somehow, the cut had stitches. Then my skin received more cuts and more stitches, and I began to bleed. I was bleeding all over the floor. The pain began to grow even worse from my fifteenth stitch to my forty-third stitch, and finally, I had eighty-five stitches all over my body from head to toe. Then the floor became a bloodbath, and I could see my reflection.

To my horror, I saw my skin half gone, and there was more meat than skin. My fingers looked all saggy. My legs looked like spider legs, and my face became sticky and wet like Play-Doh in a bowl filled with water.

While all this was happening, I could feel what was left of my skin burning. It was one of the most agonizing feelings I had ever felt, so much so I bent to the floor, screaming. But while bending, I could feel my bones, and then I heard a horrible crack. I realized that it was my back breaking. Then I fell to the floor, and my back broke completely onto the floor. It must have twisted the spinal cord, along with the nerves. The whole thing…well, it was just too horrible to describe.

But I could say, when all this was happening and with all the chaos that was going on during whatever the hell that was, I began to stop laughing; and finally, I began to scream. It was so loud it was echoing everywhere around the pit I fell through. It was so loud, in fact, it was even more painful than my own physical pain and anguish because, at that moment, I had inside myself out.

About twenty-eight seconds later, I could hear voices saying, "James! James!" While hearing this, I closed my eyes for about three seconds and finally opened them up.

But nothing happened, so I yelled, "Help!"

Then I was finally out of the pit. But when I came back, I wasn't back at the statehouse but someplace else. I didn't know what it was, but I could see myself with a straitjacket and with hospital guards. I said to myself, *What the hell just happened?*

While all this was going on, I realized some doctor was next to me.

When I saw him, I was doing it. But at the same time, I knew it didn't matter. All that mattered was to figure out where Celia and the rebels were.

About a few minutes later, the doctor looked at me and said, "You're okay, son?"

"I don't know… Where am I?"

"You're in the hospital."

Then I rolled my eyes and tried to get up, saying, "I don't have time for this!" But I fell to the floor because of the stupid straitjacket. Kyle told me that I needed to calm down, but I basically told him to go to hell.

"What's your problem, James?"

"My problem? Celia is endangered."

"What are you talking about?"

Then I sighed and explained to him that a gal named Linda Smith was after her.

Then he looked at me in shock and said, "Jesus Christ!"

"Yeah, and you better tell me where I am, or I'm going to head-butt you!"

"James!" said Kyle.

"What?"

"You're home!"

I knew what he meant, but I couldn't believe that the place I was in wasn't Smart City but in Kansas City, close to Tomahawk Street—where I used to live.

My face began to turn red, and I yelled out to Kyle, "Who sent me here?"

"A lady…"

"What lady?" I said.

"Blond and elderly, with a red jumpsuit."

"You stupid fool. That's Linda Smith!"

"Oh god!"

"Yeah, oh god, and by the way, how the hell did she know that I lived here once?"

"I don't know."

Then I was thinking about who might have known I lived here and knew about my past. Then suddenly I could remember the man in black saying that he knew me, but to my eyes, I thought he was delusional. Guess not. So he decided to put me far away from home to hurt the ones I loved.

I then said to Kyle I needed to leave, but he explained to me that I couldn't leave because of a big hole in my arm.

So I said, "Look, Celia is endangered, and I don't care what I'll do to get out of here. I need to save her please."

"We are never going to see each other again, right?"

"I don't know…but please don't tell my dad or Karla."

"What! Why?"

"I'm not their James anymore… Kyle, please."

While Kyle looked desperate to choose between his job or his friends, he decided to make an exception. He let me go and told me, "Okay. Just promise me that you two will be safe."

"Sure, man."

But before I was about to leave, I realized that I didn't have a car, so I turned to him and asked, "Can you drive me back?"

"Sorry, man, I'm kind of in the middle of things, but I can send you somebody."

"Who?" I said.

"I'll send one of our neurosurgeons."

"What's the name of the doctor?"

"Joseph Chung."

Chapter 13

The Rescue

It had been ten years since my mother's death, and I had been trying to do the best I could to suck it up and be a good person. Yet I felt like an imposter every time I tries because each time my mind told me something else when I tried to let go of the past. I might be well now, writing this to whoever is reading, but to say I was happy would be a lie. I was happy but angry.

While I was with Dr. Chung, driving back to Smart City, I began to ask him what happened to me, and he replied, "You are heavily wounded."

"What do you mean?" I said.

"Don't you remember?"

I started to look at my arm. I realized that something was terribly wrong because I couldn't remember what happened or who did it. Of course, it was Linda Smith, but in that moment, all I could remember was being knocked out by the man in black.

I then asked Dr. Chung, "Who did this?"

"Only you would know, sir."

"But I don't remember."

"You should."

"Please just tell me what happened."

He explained to me that a couple were saying that they found me going insane in the streets of Kansas. Later the doctors tried to restrain me, but my heart stopped. They were about to take me into the morgue when suddenly I woke up with a straitjacket on me.

I asked him, "Why would I go insane?"

"I don't know. It could be trauma? Schizophrenia? Or, hell, maybe Flakka? Then I started to have a few images popped in my head: a syringe, spitting, and screaming. I was thinking about those images, which could have been for minutes, because after having those flashes, I began to hear the car honking.

Dr. Chung said to me, "Sir, you're here!"

I began to feel confused and stunned, but I decided to shake it off and went on my way. I said to him, "Thanks."

"Wait."

I began to feel even more stunned when he called me, then I asked him, "What is it?"

"What do you mean, what is it? I drove you here, and I got nothing back?"

"I'm sorry. I got no money."

"Well, you wanna ride, you have to pay!"

I began to get aggravated, but I tried to keep calm so it wouldn't escalate to fighting.

"Look, I'll pay you tomorrow."

Then he started laughing at me because he worked all the way at Kansas.

"You make me laugh." He began to instigate further and further until a part of me just snapped.

I went straight at him with my hands, grabbing his throat, trying to choke the life out of him, saying, "Why should I pay you a cent!"

He looked at me, horrified, and started to scream for help. But that only fueled my anger, and I started to choke him harder. But then I'd realized what I was doing and let go of him. He then drove away immediately, and I started to feel guilty afterward.

Then about nine minutes later, I walked all over the streets to find where everyone was, but I couldn't find them. I even yelled out their names.

"Celia, Sarah, McNally, Dr. Barton, anybody!"

Then I saw an abandoned factory, and I could hear screams coming from there. I ran to it to check it out. When I got to it, I could see people guarding it who appeared to be armed. While looking closer, the factory became somewhat familiar to me. Then I saw a window; and even though it was far away, I could recognize what was inside there, but I couldn't have the images in my head yet… until I did. I realized that was the place where I was tortured, but with what? While all this was happening, I could hear the screams again; and while I was closer, I tried to find a way to get in, but the place was heavily guarded by people in red jumpsuits, but with military suits on them. I thought they were the senate, but they appeared bulkier and colder, and I didn't know where to go. Then the screams appeared from the window, and I found out who they were, and I was repulsed.

I immediately rushed in until I saw a guard coming. I bend down in the blink of an eye. While the guards were blocking the way, I then saw a sniper on my right and one on top of the factory. I knew I had to plan, so I tried to get my pistol until I realized how much of an idiot I was for losing it back at Kansas.

So I made another plan without a weapon. I had to get one by taking the guard out with my hands. I thought I was insane, but this world was also insane. So I approached the guard's assault rifle, but while I was about to get it, I saw a huge knife. I decided to grab the knife. While he was confused, I stabbed him in the head and grabbed his gun. I saw him on the ground with his red jumpsuit and thought, *There's an idea!* I did the most humorous thing ever. I switched jumpsuits with him while he was unconscious. And so I felt like I didn't need to do anything but just have a gun and a knife.

I walked down the hill and saw the guards, but I tried to not let guards see me really well. But there was one problem. They were blocking the door, and I tried to make a stupid-looking face so they wouldn't recognize me.

They asked me who I was, but I made them look stupid by saying, "Are you questioning my authority against the leader?"

Afterward they let me in, and I saw a bunch of meetings taking place on different sides of the factory. I also saw a green table, which was strange because everything else they wore was red, except whoever that creep in black was. I came up with an idea of what the green table represented, and it was not a pretty imagination. I thought to myself, *They are treating our fate like gambling!* While I was thinking this, I could hear the screams from downstairs, yelling, "Help! Help!"

Then I rushed down, yet a senator with a guard next to him said, "Where are you going!"

"To shut them up."

Until about three seconds, they let go, saying, "All right. Make them shut up."

While I was walking down, they stopped me again, saying, "Hey, don't forget your keys," which the senator had in his hand so no one except the senate and especially Linda Smith could go in without their permission.

I took the keys and went downstairs. My hands were shaking uncontrollably until about eighteen seconds later. I opened the door, and to my disgust, I saw everybody—from my team to the woman I loved being naked and brutalized. I gasped and almost snapped in anger, but I rushed into Celia's arm, who was blindfolded.

I said to her, "Celia! Celia!"

"James, is that you?"

"Yes, it's me!"

"Oh, good god, thank you!"

"I'm going to get you guys out of here!" I took out the ropes from the chairs to their wrists, and I can hear Sarah saying, "You came back!"

"Of course."

Then McNally and Dr. Barton said, "I almost thought you'll never come back!"

While I was loosening them up, I tried to find their jumpsuits. I then realized they were locked up in the closet, and I saw the sleeve out of the closet. So I grabbed them and told them to dress up while they were taking off their blindfolds. We all decided to get out from the window.

While we were getting out, I heard footsteps coming down, and I yelled, "Go. I'll take care of them!"

Then suddenly the door slammed and broke out, and nobody was here, except me and Linda Smith, along with the senate and the guards pointing guns at me.

Smith yelled out, "That's as far as you're going!"

They all laughed at me. I wondered to myself, *How can these people live with themselves? How can they have any soul by doing what they're doing, by torturing, brutalizing, and acting out in the most disgusting way possible, especially when they tortured Celia, and now they are laughing without remorse. But to just take me out and everyone else to stop the revolution. If they think people deserved this, so should they.*

I smiled at them and said, "You people got some balls for doing what you're doing because I'm going to beat them out of you."

They looked at me like I was cocky.

Smith said to me, "Shut up, peasant!"

In about three seconds, they pulled the trigger, and so did I. Then I blacked out.

I remembered very little of what happened after the shot was fired, but I did recall a gut feeling, like a part of me was released. I wasn't completely sure where this gut feeling came from. But I knew it was something beyond me.

After I blacked out, I woke up, gasping, in a cell. I thought it belonged to Smith.

I yelled, "Get me out of here!" And trust me, I hated my voice echoing around the cell. I yelled a second time, saying, "Who are you? Get me out of here!"

Then I heard footsteps coming down, and I began to creep out a little bit. Then I heard a voice saying, "What's wrong?"

"Who are you, and what do you mean, what's wrong!" Then the man came down. I realized it was Mark Talbot.

"Where am I, Talbot?"

"What do you mean, James?"

"WHERE AM I?"

"You told me to put you here so you can relax."

"No, I didn't."

"Whatever, kid. I'm just saying what you said. Everybody wants to thank you."

I began to look at him, very confused, until he said to me, "Are you sure you're going to be okay, kid?"

"Yeah… I think."

But I wouldn't be in the end. The consequences of not telling them what was going on until I figured out ruined me. Talbot and I went upstairs. I was a little nervous, but I decided to go along with it.

When I made it in, I saw everybody—Celia, Sarah, McNally, Dr. Barton, and the rest of the resistance—clapping for me, yelling, "Surprise!" I smiled and began to shake hands and give hugs to the people who gave me a second chance, even to start a party with them.

I was having the time of my life for about three hours into the party because they said I killed Linda Smith. When I first heard this, I was shocked and confused, but still, I went along with it.

While I was thanking everyone for their kindness, I decided to give a speech in front of the crowd.

"You guys gave me hope in a hopeless world. You give me peace in a world with violence, and Talbot, you gave a runaway kid from the streets who was lost to become something great. Who was alone and was miserable, yet that kid never asked… How can I repay you?"

I saw Talbot start to cry, and I heard him say with a soft voice, "You already did, kid."

"How?"

"Because we're in this together."

"Always."

"Always."

Then the party was over

Chapter 14

The Disc

We all walked back to our cars—McNally, Celia, Talbot, even me—until I felt a tap on my shoulder, and I turned, and it was Sarah.

I said to her, "Yeah, Sarah?"

"I would like to tell you something."

"I'm sorry, Sarah. Celia is waiting for me."

"Then here."

I received a disc. I said to her, "What is this?"

"Remember that time I yelled to Toameh."

"You were angry?

"Yeah, but you never hear me scream in Spanish."

Then I knew what she meant, but Celia was yelling, "James, comes on!"

I then said to Sarah, "Okay, I'll check it out."

"Bye, James."

"Bye, Sarah."

After what happened, it was my first day not in my house but in a hotel room after the explosion. Celia went to work, and I waved her goodbye. About three seconds later, out of curiosity, I saw the disc next to the table. I told Celia I didn't know what it was. I guessed what it could be, but I didn't want to be right.

I put the disc inside our laptop and started to play it for about three minutes. It wouldn't start. I was tapping on my finger over and over until I saw the screen pop up, and I saw green letters like in the *Matrix* films on the screen. I thought to myself, *Sarah, what the hell?*

Two minutes later

After witnessing the video, it made my stomach turn, and I couldn't believe it. I didn't want to believe it. I decided to drive off to meet Sarah myself so it came from her mouth.

I rushed to go inside Sarah's house so I could confirm this from her own mouth. I knocked on the door. About ten seconds in, nobody answered. I was about to knock again when suddenly the door opened, and I saw Dr. Barton.

He then asked me, "Hello, Mr. Truman. What are you doing here?"

"Dr. Barton, I would like to speak to your wife."

"What's wrong?"

"Nothing's wrong."

Then he looked at me like I was lying and said, "Sir, I'm a psychologist that's being transferred to another hospital and knows a lie when he sees one."

I decided to give in and said, "Sarah gave me a disc before I left."

"What was it?"

Before I was about to say anything, Sarah came and said to Dr. Barton, "It's okay, honey. Let him in."

I went inside and asked Sarah if we could step outside. She seemed to know that this was going to happen, and I decided to say it straight to her.

"You're an illegal?"

"James… I—"

"Why didn't you tell me?"

After asking her the truth that she was an illegal, she started to have a long face and said, "Look, I'm sorry. It wasn't easy for me to tell you."

"But now it is?"

"James, please!"

"You know, I don't know what to call you anymore or know if you have more secrets."

"No, there's no more. I told you everything."

"But I thought, as a friend, you would tell me the truth face-to-face."

"I would."

"But you didn't."

Then suddenly we heard sounds that sounded like firecrackers until, about two seconds later, we realized they were bullets being sprayed around. We ducked to the floor and started to hear a voice from the streets that sounded like a witch.

Both me and Sarah said quietly, "Smith!"

After realizing it was Linda Smith, Sarah turned to me in anger, yelling, "I thought you killed that dictator!"

"I did."

"But you didn't."

I was shocked after hearing what I said Sarah being told back to me, but I knew I probably deserved it.

Afterward we rushed to catch it. We went up, all the way straight, with our guns ready to aim. For a moment, we thought we had her. But when we were running, Sarah turned, and I followed her trail until we were surprised by Linda Smith, along with the senate and the guards surrounding us.

She told us to drop our guns, then she looked at me, saying, "Nice to see you, D."

"D?"

"Oh, I forgot. You're Mr. Goody Two-shoes. Well, let me explain. It's short for Devil."

Then Sarah looked at her and looked at me then finally put the pieces together before I did and understood why I looked shocked when Smith appeared. She asked Smith, "What did you do to my friend?"

Smith started grinning and said, "Nice to see you knowing the answer, Barton."

Sarah squeezed her fist as if she was going to punch her. Then I told her to calm down because Smith and everyone had guns pointed right at us.

"You better listen to your friend, Barton," said Smith.

Then we saw everybody looking at us with a dark grin on their faces.

Sarah became furious and started yelling, "This is all your fault—for the death and torment of many lives: Jackson, Mendez, Nabeel, and James. I swear I will also suffer and die also." Then Sarah was slapped down to the floor. And the way she was slapped triggered what happened to me, not just one memory but every other memory returning.

I began to gasp and said to myself, "I remember… I remember everything… You. And that man in black… You two did this to me!"

"Finally, you remember." Then she pointed their weapons at me. Smith then said to me, "Now die."

I closed my eyes, and the shot was fired…but not at me. At her.

Madame Linda Smith, leader of Smart City, was shot in the throat by a gun. Everybody from her group had their jaws dropped. They all looked around, including me. Then I turned around and saw a blurry look of a man with a sniper rifle, and I realized it was Mark Talbot who took the shot. And with him was my family—the rebels.

It turned out Sarah was never unconscious; she just called Talbot and the rebels for one last blood war. They all rushed in, both the rebels and the senators with their guards. I was so excited. Too bad I didn't see all of it. Turned out the drug Flakka was taking its effect on me. I ran so no one could get hurt. I was hiding in a corner, hearing the shots being fired and people screaming. It must have been as bloody as the movie *Hacksaw Ridge*. Then, while in the corner, a rebel made a huge mistake. He tapped me in the back, saying, "Are you okay?"

But the last words I could remember were me yelling, "Playtime!"

Then he tried to run away. It was the last time he'd ever run again. After that, I blacked out.

After I'd blacked out, I remembered waking up and seeing myself in a white room with a straitjacket on. I thought to myself, *What the hell is this?* Then I saw in front of me a door with a square glass window, and the people there were Celia, Dr. Barton, Sarah, McNally, Talbot, and the rest of the rebels.

I asked them, "What did you do?"

"Is that you, James?" asked Dr. Barton.

"Yes, it's me. Who else can it be?"

They began to talk to themselves like, "He doesn't remember," and "The drug is even worse than we thought."

"Hey, guys, stop talking to yourself, and start talking to me on why I am here."

"James, you seriously don't remember?" said Talbot.

"Remember what?" I said.

"You're in Blackstone Penitentiary. You've been here for two weeks."

I began to feel chills down my spine, realizing I was in a medical center for the sick, a kind of even sicker rehab.

"You can't be serious!"

"I'm sorry, James, but after Smith was killed, you…um…"

"What?"

"You've… You killed a man, James," said Sarah.

I looked at my hands and couldn't believe it. I thought this was some sort of prank until I saw all their faces—from Sarah to McNally, Talbot, and even Celia and Dr. Barton.

"How?" I yelled.

"It was the drug," said McNally.

"What are you talking about?"

"When you got tortured by Smith and her henchmen, one of them injected you with Flakka."

"I…um…"

The memories were starting to pop up, but they were so painful I refused to relive them, except the injection.

"You remember anything, James?" said Dr. Barton.

"A man…a man in black injected me with the drug!"

"What kind of man? Was he White, Black, Asian, Hispanic?"

"I don't know!"

"What do you mean you don't know?" said Talbot.

"I don't know. His face was covered."

"Okay. We will look for him. Okay, James."

"But what about me?"

"James, you're too dangerous right now, and we need to make a plan to help you," said Dr. Barton.

Then I got furious and banged my head against the glass window and yelled, "Who asked you?"

"Celia did, James," said Dr. Barton.

"What… Is this true?"

"James, look, I just heard what those monsters did to you, but this isn't forever."

Then I was distraught that after everything that happened, I was going to be in this place.

"James, you're NOT crazy, and this isn't only a mental hospital. It's both medical and mental," Celia said.

I turned my body backward, toward the wall, and Dr. Barton said, "James. It's not over. I will keep on searching for what is causing you to change, then you'll go free, and my wife will find the man responsible for your condition."

Even thought he was trying to help, I was feeling too helpless and powerless to care. I said to him, "No, she won't. Get out!"

"James," said Dr. Barton.

"Get out, all of you, out!" I yelled.

Then I heard footsteps of all those who were the people I knew, leaving me alone, and how alone I was. Then I put my head down, like I was bowing, for about three minutes until I heard a voice came of nowhere, yelling, "Fool!"

"Who's there?" I said.

"The one thing living that came out of the drug…a demon!"

"Oh my god!"

Chapter 15

Blackstone Penitentiary

It was my first day at Blackstone Penitentiary, and I could tell you that it wasn't a pleasant experience, especially that I came out of the white room, which happened to be solitary confinement.

About 12:34 a.m. I was sent to a room so they could take my photograph. I was forced to put on a white jumpsuit to blend in with the other patients. I was given a number, and that was what I was to them—just a number they gave me—not James Truman but number 032097.

I was led to my room, with security guards monitoring my every move. My bed was next to some guy with dreadlocks and a goatee, but unlike him, he was fast asleep, and I was having trouble sleeping. While in bed, I started to have memories of Celia, of how strong she was to not give up on me…until now. I wasn't angry at her, but I was angry at myself.

I continued not to sleep for about thirty minutes until a bald security guard said to me with a cold voice, "Go to sleep!"

I explained to him that I couldn't. He then told me to get up. I was then led back to solitary confinement, and trust me, I did not want to go back into that hole.

"Get in!" he said.

"I can think of ten good reasons to not get in!"

"Well…"

Immediately I was thrown into solitary. I was on the floor, turning my head, and the guard told me, "You think you rule there, but you don't rule here."

As if he knew me. Instead of fighting the bald jerk, I just didn't care anymore. I looked out the window and saw bars covering it in case someone tried to commit suicide. I spent about five hours there, with my face looking at the window, with my feet feeling numb. While in solitary, I wanted to see everybody I knew again, and about one hour more, I fell asleep.

Then about ten or fifth teen minutes later, everyone was told to wake up, including me. I was told by a small middle-aged man with glasses.

I then said to him while I was in solitary, "Who are you?"

He looked at me with a strange smile and said, "My name is Claude Mitchell."

"And what else are you?"

"I'm the director of Blackstone Penitentiary."

While he was talking, I was looking for that bald bastard who threw me out so I could snitch on him, but he wasn't there.

"Where is he?"

"Who?"

"The bald-headed security guard!"

"You mean Mr. Barber?"

"Whatever!"

"He took the day off. Why do you want to know about him?"

I was about to speak when suddenly I was surprised by a familiar face, Dr. Patrick Barton.

"Dr. Barton?"

"James, I…"

I was about to jump on him, but I was restrained by Mitchell. When I was getting tougher, he was yelling at me to stop.

I then said, "He put me in here in the first place!"

"So what are you going to do to, kill him! Or he can find an antidote for you."

I was stunned and said, "What?"

Then Dr. Barton said to me, "It's true, James, but it's a chance also, yet it might take me a few days to make it happen."

"What is it?"

He then explained to me with just three words: "A blood transfusion."

After hearing that I might be healed through a blood transfusion, I was asked if I wanted to see a visitor.

I looked at Mr. Mitchell and said "Yes."

I was then led to my room, with Dr. Barton and Mr. Mitchell. While walking, I was thinking about who the visitor might be. About ten seconds later, I thought about it until I saw her. It was Celia. I was happy at first until about two seconds later. I was able to see her in a way that was unexpected to me. I was ashamed to have her look at me like a madman. But somehow, she didn't see me like that at all.

When I went to her, she looked at me and said with a tiny smile, "How are you doing?"

I lied to her to make her feel better by saying, "I'm just hanging in there." I thought to myself, *Why does this have to happen to me?* I then asked her, "Did Sarah figure out who and what made me this way?"

"Sarah said that this lunatic in black could be middle age and six feet tall."

I smiled at her, and we began to speak about many things, but one of the first things we did was kiss.

Chapter 16

Solitary Confinement

After Celia had left, I was at my room and was thinking to myself over and over about her and how much I would love to see her again, yet at the same time, I also thought, *Will Dr. Barton help me get rid of this crap in my blood?*

Then a roommate of mine looked at me and said, "Nice whore. Maybe when I find a way out of here, I'll take her!" His name was Number 032098, or in the outside world, Brendan Johnson. He was once an informant for the State to take out an undercover member of the rebels named John Clay. After killing Clay, he later went off into the woods, never to be seen again until now.

By the time he called and insulted Celia and threatened to escape so he could have his way with her, I became so furious I grabbed Johnson by the neck and started throwing punches at him. I then heard footsteps running toward my cell, and it was two guards, the bald jerk who threw me to solitary and another one with a goofy hairdo. I was then body-slammed to the floor and was forced to wear another damn straitjacket. The more I tried to break out, the more they began to squeeze my arms on me. I was later thrown not in solitary but in an interrogation room

When I was inside, nobody came to talk to me for thirty-eight minutes. But then I heard Mr. Mitchell calling me in a loud voice, "Number 032097, do you know where you are?"

"Yes, sir," I said

"Do you know why you are here?"

"Yes, sir."

He then approached me, with glasses almost close to my face, saying, "Then you know that you had a crisis with one of our patients."

"I was angry."

"And that makes it okay?"

"I don't need your opinions."

Then Mr. Mitchell looked at me with a straight face and said with a cold voice right at me, "Well, I don't need yours. Keep this up, and you'll be put in solitary."

I began to feel offended by Mitchell's tone. I then threw a series of profanities at him, and he was also offended. He then asked the guards to escort me to solitary confinement.

They picked me up, and one of them said, "I told you, you don't rule here!"

While I was solitary, I hadn't said a word for at least an hour. In solitary, I was sweating and hated myself and the guards, but not as much as that black-masked thug who injected me with that poison and turned me into Dr. Jekyll and Mr. Hyde. If only I could see him now. I would strangle him, and sometimes I did dream of me strangling him, but not as myself but as my darker self.

While in solitary, I could hear a voice, and it was slowly getting louder and louder. I tried to cover my ears until I realized I could still hear it. I thought I was going mad.

But then the voices stopped. I closed my eyes when suddenly I heard a voice again, but this time, it just said one word. "Look at you!"

I then looked around and said, "Who's there?"

I tried to see who was there, yet I couldn't see anything. But I knew he saw me. I walked around in solitary, saying, "Who are you!"

"You idiot! You mean who am I?"

"Who are you calling an idiot?"

Then, out of nowhere, I could feel a strange feeling from behind me. I turned, and I realized it was my shadow. But then it started to have a life of its own. It grabbed me and picked me up by the neck while choking me.

I finally recognized the person who was hiding. It was my enemy.

"You piece of trash!" My eyes started to become blurred, and I felt like I was going to die. I struggled to get out.

"You think I'm a piece of trash? Sure, I'm a twisted maniac, but it's not my fault. Nobody asked you to run away from your father and sister, who are probably are suffering for the past ten years. Nobody asked you to stay in Smart City with your own girlfriend, who had even begged you to come back to your family. Nobody asked you to join those damn revolutionaries that led you to become two people, that led you to be put in this hellhole for God knows how long, and I'm a piece of trash?"

"Why are you telling me this?"

"To prove a point. You're no saint, and you're no Jekyll. You just a half-minded, stubborn piece of crap."

"Yeah, well, you're not real!" When I said that while being choked, D smiled and began twitching and began to punch me in the chin.

"Did that feel real?"

I began to shake around, with my teeth gnashing, while trying to escape. And for about five seconds, I was screaming until it ended with me realizing I was choking myself.

In about six days after the incident, I was finally released. I felt so damn misused. I was then sent to the lunchroom, where all the other patients were. I thought to myself, *Why am I not in my room?*

While they were serving me my food, I saw a crazy guy with sharp teeth and a mohawk looking at me with so much hate. He was Number 042100. But in society, he was named Henry Lombardi.

I thought to myself, *What is this wacko's problem?* While a few steps from having my lunch, he came to me and slammed my plate to the floor, and nobody, not even the guards, did anything about it. Later it turned out that he had connections with big people outside Smart City that blackmailed the guards if they wouldn't follow him. With him achieving power in Blackstone, he was untouchable.

After having my food slammed to the floor, he started looking at me with a smug face, saying, "Today you're mine."

I had my head down without saying a word while hoping he would leave me alone soon. But instead, he instigated over and over, and I was still silent, without a word from my mouth. Then about two or three insults later, he mentioned someone.

"Who's Celia?"

I looked up and started to breath heavily.

"Oh, there he is. Well, you don't mind if I could find out."

I began to twitch, and my face and eyes became burning red.

"Well, if you would stand here, I would just find out when I get out of here and teach her how to be happy."

My teeth began to gnash, and my hands began to shake. I was so angry. A lot of people that saw me said I had the face of the specter of death. I was sweating, shaking, and with a disturb look, with bloodshot eyes almost coming out of its sockets. I went up and punched the psycho in the face. But he turned and looked at me with just a small, bloody lip.

He smiled and said, "Is that your best?" Then he punched me in the forehead and put me to the ground. Then he came to me with a bloody face.

"Who the hell do you think you're slapping at, huh, who? Yeah, that's right. I just own your punk ass!"

Chapter 17

The Doctor

I never felt so pulverized. The way I hit felt like getting hit by a boulder. All I could remember was darkness for about ten or twelve seconds until I heard my name being called repeatedly over and over by someone that I thought was my dad.

"James? James?" Then, in the blink of an eye, the voice yelled out, "Don't make me kill you!"

I gasped and jumped up and felt something all over my head. I then saw a half-broken mirror, and I could see bandages covering my head, like it was burned or something. I then realized it was because of that piece of crap.

I then tried to get up, but I saw a doctor coming to me, saying, "Number 032097, please relax!"

"Where am I?"

"You're in the infirmary."

I then started to touch my head, but an aching feeling came from it, like a vein being squished.

"Sir, please, you're very injured." I then asked the doctor her name, and she said, "My name is Dr. Rosa Bernstein."

I smiled and said, "Are you German?"

"Actually, I'm Jewish."

I was stunned a bit and said, "Oh… Well, my mother's Jewish."

Dr. Bernstein said to me with a very friendly smile, "What's your mother's name?"

While we were talking, the bald-headed guard came and spoke with a loud voice, asking for me, but Dr. Bernstein said, "Mr. Barber, my patient isn't ready yet."

"I understand, but it's a request from Dr. Patrick Barton."

I turned to Dr. Bernstein and said, "It's okay, Doc, I know Dr. Barton." I then got up, with my head feeling like it was filled with stitches, and was led with the guard next to me inside a room; and finally, after ten days since my first time in Blackstone, I saw Dr. Barton.

"Hello, James. Sit."

I remained still and refused to speak because I felt like he failed me. He then asked me how I was doing, but I just shrugged it off and continued to be silent.

He then looked at me very sadly and said, "James, I know you're angry, but please understand. We put you here to help you." But I kept being silent. He then spoke again and said, "James… I never lied to you about the treatment that can heal you."

I finally answered him, saying, "The others here don't seem to care about it or me."

"Some do!" said Dr. Barton.

"They think I'm a lost cause."

Dr. Barton then said to me with a sad look on his face, "Is that so?"

"It sure is," I said.

"James, remember I am here for you."

"Sure, you are!" Then Dr. Barton's professional nature broke a second time since he was in Life's Garden. He slammed the desk and said, "Quit your bitching and moaning!" While realizing what he just did, he became shocked and apologized to me with a very serious look on his face, but I didn't care.

"I'm sorry," said Dr. Barton.

"Well, I'm not."

Then I went up and was about to leave the room. I began to open the door when suddenly the guard came and held me by the arms, then I began to struggle to find a way out.

Patrick stepped up, saying, "Hey, he's not in a crisis. Let him go!"

"But, Doctor!" said the guard.

"Let him go!"

I was finally released from that thug's arms. I then saw Dr. Barton looking at me with guilt.

He then said, "You may go back to your room, James." I was about to walk out until Patrick spoke again and said, "James, wait!"

I turned around and said, "Yeah?"

"Don't look so sad."

I then felt agitated and said, "Why shouldn't I be?"

Dr. Barton then said with a sad smile, "Just have a little faith because together we are going to fix this…okay?"

I then shrugged my shoulders and said, "Okay."

"Good, because in two weeks, we will figure out what's wrong and heal you."

I thought about it and nodded my head, saying, "Okay, Doc."

Then the guard showed me to my room, and I then fell asleep.

Then about two hours later, I was still in my bed. I'd been hoping for Dr Barton to get rid of this evil out of my system. But I didn't know if I could wait for two weeks; even thinking about it could make me go nuts. I didn't know what to do. All I had in my mind was, I needed to get out of here; so at midnight, I'd made a choice. Whether it was a good or bad one didn't matter anymore because I'd made a choice to end this nightmare.

I began to feel very emotional, but I refused to express it. I got up out of my bed and went to the bathroom. I then started to look at my reflection for about five seconds until I finally expressed at least half of what I felt. I was angry, so angry, in fact, I slammed my head against the mirror over and over. I then saw blood sticking on the mirror.

Then the bald guard came and held me to the neck while I fell headfirst to the toilet and began to try to scratch the guy's face while he was holding me. Each time I tried, my neck started to feel crushed. I tried to break loose, but there was no point. After about fifteen seconds on the floor, I thought the guard hit me until I realized that it was a syringe being injected on the thigh. I felt as though I was kicked by a horse. I began to gasp, and about five seconds later, I was knocked out.

Chapter 18

The Antidote

I've never thought things could get worse after being in solitary, but to be touched by a group of brutes over and over… Well, that was something even I in this godforsaken hospital could not foresee. I really wanted Dr. Barton to get rid of this demon in me. Because I didn't know how long I could last.

I felt myself getting squeezed from the inside every time I smelled this cesspool I was in. I would say to myself every day, "So this is the hell my dad told me to go."

While having all this out, I saw myself being restrained on a bed. I'd realized I was once again in the infirmary, and this time, I saw not one but three doctors, whose names were Dr. Veronica Charles, Dr. Peg Ravo, and Dr. Barbara Ruth.

One of them went to me and said, "Good morning, sunshine."

"Who are you?"

"We are Dr. Barton's assistants," said Dr. Charles.

I then asked Dr. Ravo if I could go back to my room, and she replied, "Of course."

While I was getting up, another doctor named Dr. Ruth spoke up and said, "Number 032097?"

"Yes?" I said.

"Dr. Barton will be seeing you tomorrow."

I then smiled and said, "Thank you."

I was sent to my room and couldn't sleep because I wanted to get rid of the drug from my system. I sometimes thought to myself while in my room what I didn't really say to anyone, which was, *How would my mom see me today?* Would she see her poor James or just a disappointment? While in my room, I began to think about my sister, Celia, and even my own dad. So many thoughts from them were in my head, in time, I later fell asleep and began to dream.

I started remembering my mom—how sweet she was to me, how her kind smile was that of an angel, how I could never forget the love she showed me. But then my dream became a nightmare from hell.

I was a kid. One evening, my mom was dressing up for our thanksgiving dinner with the whole family. I realized she was taking too long, but nobody dared to disturb her, not even my dad.

But then I went upstairs, knocking the door, and I couldn't see what was going on, but it sounded like she was coughing heavily. I looked at the keyhole when suddenly I saw her coughing blood. I freaked out and started screaming.

I came downstairs to tell everyone what happened, but they all were too drunk to understand. Some of them treated it like a joke, and some of them were abusive both physically and verbally.

Then I went to my dad, and he was also drunk. I tried to explain to him what was happening to mom, but he didn't take it seriously. I tried again, but he slapped me in the face, and I fell to the floor while everyone, including my dad, were laughing and pointing at me. Then I saw Karla hiding under the kitchen table while everyone was drunk; she was so scared. With no one to help me, I ran back to check on my mom, and I started to kick on the door. My dad came up and was red-faced angry.

He started yelling at me while holding my arm, "Don't make me kill you!"

While hearing Mom coughing, he then came to his senses and slammed the door down, but it was too late. My mom was dead. We found out later her brain was swollen by drinking cyanide. The doctors believed it was suicide, but the cops were convinced that she was murdered.

While taking this all in, I yelled to my dad, "It's your fault Mom is dead! It's your fault Mom is dead!"

While I was dreaming, these words kept repeating over and over, and it got louder and louder. I then started to have a gut feeling from my dark side. About three or five seconds later, I woke up, and the voices started to come back stronger, saying things like, "You're nothing! You're weak, You're pathetic! You cannot escape me! You cannot stop me! You cannot beat me!" Then it got worse when the voices started to laugh at me and taunt me. "You fool, I am your god, and I will follow you wherever you go!"

Then he threatened to take my life. "I'm going to kill you! I'm going to eat you!" It just kept going on and on until I finally just couldn't take it anymore. I began to sweat and gnash my teeth. Until I finally opened my eyes and screamed so loud my voice echoed throughout the entire hospital. Then about five to ten seconds later, I slowly blacked out.

It must have been about thirty minutes later because I was out of my cell, and to make matters worse, all the patients were next to me, saying, "What kind of monster are you?"

"What are you talking about?" I said.

Then suddenly I felt a sharp pinch on my arm, and automatically, I looked to see what was wrong. It was Dr. Barton carrying a sedative in his hand.

I began to feel light-headed, but not enough to see what my other half did. I could see the bald-headed guard on the floor, with his head bleeding to the ground.

The last words I said before being put back to sleep were, "Oh god!"

Then Dr. Barton whispered to my ear, "It's time, James."

After I was put to sleep again in that godforsaken place, I began dreaming about the guard. Yes, he was a bully, but I was not a bloodthirsty killer; and even if he did deserve it, it should never be by me because nobody needed to see the worst of me, including my worst enemies.

While all this was happening, I began to feel very weak and tired because of the anesthetic. My eyes were looking at the ceiling and were half shut. For twenty minutes, I heard doctors talking to each other. I couldn't understand what they were saying because the door was shut. But I did hear things like, "Flakka" and "new blood." They might have been asking what would happen, but I couldn't hear well.

While waiting and looking at the ceiling, I saw a man with brown hair that resembled an executive. He had a huge mustache. I realized it was Dr. Patrick Barton.

He looked at me and said, "How are you doing, James?"

But I ignored the question and said, "Is the guard okay?"

Dr. Barton sighed and said, "He is recovering, James."

I put my hands on my face and said, "What have I done?"

"It wasn't your fault."

"You know…almost that was true, Doc."

Dr. Barton smiled and said, "You know why you came here, right?"

"Yeah, I guess."

"You are here to prevent that from happening again before it's too late."

"What do you mean?"

He explained to me that if I didn't have an antidote into my body, there was a huge possibility that I would get worse.

"How is that possible, Doc?"

"The blood in your system right now is creating a split personality."

"You mean I'm turning into two people."

"Yes." Then I looked down to the floor, and he said, "James, is there something you want to tell me?"

I paused for about three minutes and said, "No, Doc."

He started to look serious and said, "You're lying, son."

I covered my face with my hands and began to confess. "All right, Doc, you got me. It's just I can hear someone talking to me."

"Who?"

And I said, "A demon."

He then held me on the shoulders and gave a sad smile while saying, "That's why you're here, and besides, I finally created an antidote."

I was shocked and said straight at him, "You did it?"

"I'm not fully sure."

"Will it heal me?"

"I don't know, but it's possible, and I need a sample right now!"

I was a little nervous, so much even Doctor Barton noticed through my expression.

About two seconds after asking for the sample, he said to me, "Don't worry, James. It's going to be fine."

I began to smile, saying, "Thank you, Doctor."

"You are very welcome."

About two minutes later, Dr. Barton took both samples and mixed them together for about thirty-three minutes. He was able to take out some of the flaws that were inside the Flakka drug and made it compatible with my blood. After almost an hour, the antidote was ready to be injected unto me.

He had a syringe and said, "Ready?"

"Yes."

"All right. Three! Two! One!" And he injected me with it.

After being injected with the antidote, I was told to go back to my room. Dr. Barton explained that I just needed to let it flow through my system, and tomorrow he would see the results along with the other doctors.

I was sent back to my room and waited the next day. When it was morning, I was told by a new guard who was substituting the bald-headed guard. Even though I hated that guy, I felt sorry for him.

While walking, I was sent to Dr. Barton's office. He then asked the guard to wait outside. But the guard insisted that it wasn't a good idea.

Dr. Barton replied, "I understand, but please understand also that he's a friend of my wife, and I trust him."

The guard nodded and went outside the office. Dr. Barton asked me to sit, and so I did. He then asked me how I was doing, to which I replied, "Can you just tell me what you found, Doc? Am I ready to go back or what?"

"I'm very confident, James."

"So you're telling me I can go?"

Dr. Barton replied, "Well, let's see how your blood type is today."

Dr. Barton then gave me a pinch on my finger, and a drop of blood came out. He then used it as a sample on the microscope to see if I was healed.

Dr. Barton then said to me, "James."

"Yeah?"

"You're healed."

Then I started jumping and dancing and making a complete fool out of myself, saying, "Yes, I'm free. Thank you, Doctor!"

But then he said one word that destroyed me, "But!"

I looked very shocked and scared, saying, "But what?"

"You're healed now…but there is a slight chance you could have Flakka return back in your blood."

I was puzzled and asked, "How?"

"The healthy cells are strong, but I don't know how strong, so for your sake, I recommend keeping you here for two weeks until we make sure you're finally free from this demon."

"So no change," I said.

"That's not what I'm saying. They are normal now. All I'm saying is, you just need to take it easy until everything is safe for yourself and everyone else."

"I don't want to take it easy. I want to be who I was!"

"Me too. All I'm saying is, you're healed, but to be sure, we need to keep you here for at least two weeks."

Then I began to answer him a question that would later be a big mistake. "You think I won't fall back down the slippery slope again, Doc?"

"I'm not sure."

"Yes, you are. How can you make something that is not a hundred percent sure?"

"James, what you got is a cure, but it needs time."

"I don't want to make time. I don't want to stay here!"

"It's just two weeks, James!"

After a few seconds, I became furious and, out of nowhere, threw things from Barton's office.

"James, calm down. The cells!" yelled Dr. Barton.

"Shut up!"

"Look at yourself. You're acting as the demon you don't want to become!"

"I said shut up!" Then I smacked him in the face, which triggered a memory of me slapping Celia from many years ago…and it also seems to have triggered Flakka back in my blood. I looked in shock, saying, "Oh no. What have I done? I'm sorry, Doc. I'm so sorry!"

Then the guard came in from outside the door and body-slammed me to the ground.

He then yelled, "I knew I shouldn't stay away from a maniac like you!"

After he said those words, I screamed and screamed and screamed!

Chapter 19

HERO TO PARIAH

I was then thrown back into solitary. It was the lowest thing in my life since I ran away ten years ago. I knew my life as a runaway was going to be bad, but I didn't expect that it was going to be this bad. For ten years, I'd failed to keep my anger under control. I'd failed to find peace, and finally, I failed to succeed. I realized, if I wanted peace, I would have sought it years ago. If I could start all over again, I would have found a way and still be who I was. It was nice to have memories before my dark side was unleashed. That life was the only thing that was close to my heart, and it became nothing but a memory, and for about one month, I had been in solitary, with crummy old food that the guards gave me. My heart became hardened, and I'd become unfeeling. I grew a small beard and had a lot of hatred and distrust toward others. I wanted to die so badly, and I didn't care if it was quick or slow because I already experienced all the pain this world had to offer.

I began to hear voices again, saying, "You weakling!"

I began to yell with a loud voice, "Shut up. This is your fault!"

"No, it's his, remember?" Then I understood that he was referring to someone, not the man in black but instead Dr. Patrick Barton.

I then replied, "Go to hell!"

Then I felt a slap on my face, and D appeared out of nowhere, yelling, "This is hell, and I'm the devil!"

Then the voices began to laugh over and over. I thought I was going crack when suddenly, to my shock, a guard opened the door and said, "You're free!"

Then he escorted me to the lunchroom, with my hands shaking. I then went to receive my lunch, with my hands still shaken. About eight seconds later it was slapped down by none other than Henri Lombardi, who was, for most patients and guards, a king. But to me he was a bully.

After he slammed my food on the floor, he looked at me and sarcastically said, "Oops!"

He saw me shaking and thought I was afraid, but I was only shaking because I was pissed. I saw Brendan Johnson on his table, eating while laughing at what Lombardi did, but not just Johnson but everyone else. This started to fuel me up, but not as much as what Lombardi said.

"I heard that Mexican slut left you. Maybe some of my boys could pick up her curvy ass and show her what a real man or men can do for her, huh, James?"

"There's only one problem," I said.

"What problem?"

"I'm not James…" Then I blacked out.

At that moment, I knew that it was too late for me to be redeemed. My life didn't matter. My history in the resistance was irrelevant. Now James David Truman was sentenced to death by my fellow rebels at the resistance. Blackstone let it happen because of the deformity of Blackstone patient Henri Lombardi, who suffered multiple physical traumas and nearly death by—you guessed it—me or, in reality, my other half.

After I blacked out, I realized D turned Henri Lombardi's face and body into a physically scared, toothless, and hideous freak; and according to those who saw me doing it, they said that I beat him so badly he began screaming, with blood splattering everywhere and on the guards' uniforms, who were yelling, "Get off him!"

One of them was that jackass who body-slammed me. He stabbed me with a syringe on my neck, and then I grabbed it and stabbed him in the eye with it, leaving him in agony, while some of the guards came to his aid, and others still tried stop me from killing Lombardi. According to Brendon Johnson, he saw me turn Lombardi backward and grab the lower part of his back by squeezing through his skin, and everyone heard a horrible crack so loud it sounded like I was twisting his spinal cord, and Lombardi began to cry. Then the guards began punching me over and over in the head, hoping to knock to me out; and another kicked me in the cheek, and I bit his leg like an animal, and I nearly chewed off another guard's finger

While all this happened, they saw me getting up while grabbing Lombardi through the neck as if I was going to break it, but then I began to feel weak, and I fell to the floor.

While I realized what happened, I asked myself, Why did this happened to me? Who would care to answer that question? I did the crime, and at somewhere, about 12:41 a.m., I would have my brain cut, leaving me brain-dead. Everyone, even my lover, Celia, considered me a lost cause. Before Celia gave me a quote from Psalm 23. After she had given me it, she left to go back to her old life. I knew in that moment I wouldn't see her again.

I was then told by the guards, the Bartons, and even McNally and Talbot, who looked at me in my room, "It's time, kid." I was escorted to a van with other lost causes. I thought a lot about Celia and wished the best for her. About two hours later, the driver drove us to the resistance hideout, which had now become a base since I left. The city became cleaner and brighter and had people for the first time without green jumpsuits. Now they wore average clothing that I heard was later found from the state of an extinct race. Everybody seemed to see the light in this world, but to me, all I saw was darkness. The van stopped, and I was led with the others to be executed. And lo and behold, I was the first one. When I went inside, a rebel gave me a sedative so I wouldn't fight back. My hair was shaved, and I was escorted to be sedated.

When I lay down, they put restraints on me. I saw in a window all the faces of everyone that were my friends and partners. I'd felt destroyed, but not as much when I saw a lady looking at me, and only me. It was Henri Lombardi's mother, looking at me with disgust, and in that moment, I felt broken.

Then I heard a voice saying, "You have anything to say?"

I then turned with a sad voice, "I…" Then suddenly, to my horror, in the window, I saw him. I saw the man in black, with the crowd of people looking at me. I yelled, "Oh my god. It's him. Get him!" Then I saw Dr. Barton, and I yelled, "Doctor, he's there. It's the guy that did this to me. Get him!" I yelled even louder, "He's right there. He's right there next to you!"

Then I saw the man in black leaving the building, but before that, Dr. Barton turned and saw the back of his body for the first time. He then looked at me and yelled, "James!" Then in a blink of an eye, out of nowhere, just as the man in black was leaving, I was in a fiery explosion!

All I could remember before the explosion went off was a huge, bright light that came from the glass. I was so terrified I believed I was going to die. When I woke up, I was on the floor, and blood was coming through my nose.

A lot of things happened during that night. I was surrounded by smoke, fire, and electricity. I tried to get up, but I realized I was still in restraints. But at the same time, because of the shock of the explosion, the sedative burned out of my system, and I could feel more active; but I knew it still didn't matter because I was going to burn unless I did something!

I tried to get out of the restraints, but one of my arms was too connected to the ropes, which made it impossible to break out the easy way. So I made a brutal choice. I broke my arm so the ropes could loosen a bit. I got out and started to find my way through to save my friends and partners. But sadly, because of my arm being damaged, I only managed to save three people: Dr. Barton, Sarah, and McNally. The rest of them—the rebels, Talbot, even Lombardi's mom—wouldn't make it.

I then ran to the woods when suddenly I was pushed to the ground, and the rest of my friends fell like rag dolls. I turned and saw the man in black. I then got up and tried to tackle him, but he then punched me on the cheek, and I fell to the ground. Then he started kicking my face over and over again to the point when my nose started to get bloody.

I then tried to reach the others, but he pulled me away by the leg and said to my surprise, "You know, I'm the only one who can fix you. Too bad you won't live for that to happen. I'll be going to Hong Kong."

Then he picked up a rock and threw it to my head, and I fell unconscious. About eleven minutes later, I woke up, and I saw everyone still on the ground and in their same position, except Dr. Barton. I came over and saw something on his head. I realized it was a knife.

"Barton!" I yelled.

Then, while feeling like my head was squeezing from the inside as if a machine was putting pressure to my head, I crawled to him and tried to pull out the knife. Blood poured out from his head.

I yelled out in horror, "Don't bleed please!"

Then I heard a voice from one of the people I saved. I turned and saw it was Sarah. She turned and saw me with the knife next to Dr. Barton, and I foolishly thought she was going to ask, "Who did this?" But my heart sunk when she said, "What have you done to my husband!"

I turned to the knife and Dr. Barton's remains and realized what she meant.

"It wasn't me, Sarah!"

I explained to Sarah, but she refused to believe me then tried to shoot me, saying, "I should have been killed after I told you the truth about who I was!"

I was stunned and heartbroken that our friendship had come to this.

"Get the hell away from my husband!"

"Sarah, I didn't do this!"

"Screw you!" Then she shot me where my arm was broken. I was in a hell of a lot of pain. The bullet felt like metal going through my bones. I then tried to escape from the woods while she was shooting at me.

I was almost to the streets, but I fell to the ground, with my damaged arm next to a log. At that moment, I decided to give him and let her kill me. I realized it was impossible for me to go on, so I waited for her to find me and shoot me. I sat down with my arm and my head swelling, with a bloody nose dripping to the dirt.

I then began to close my eyes and said, "It's over." Five seconds later, I then saw Sarah coming closer. I just didn't care anymore. So I waited…

While waiting, I heard a voice, but this time, it wasn't an evil voice but something else. And the voice sounded like someone I knew, but I had no idea who it was, but it said, "Don't give up!"

I replied to whatever or whoever it was, "There's no hope for me."

"Maybe for me, but there's always hope for the living. If you die here, then my killer wins!"

Then the voice stopped, and I realized that voice. And I decided to say to myself, *You're right, Dr. Barton… I won't give up!* Then I got up on my two legs and ran to freedom.

Behind me, I heard Sarah yelling, "James!"

I turned and said, "Goodbye, Sarah."

I then lowered my head for about five seconds and ran off and never looked back.

One year later

Now my journey began. I wrote this while visiting the graves of thirty innocent civilians who were killed by the explosion. While twenty of them survived, they suffered third-degree burns in many parts of their bodies. Four people had perished in that explosion, including Mark Talbot, Henri Lombardi, Nicole Lombardi, and yes, even Patrick Barton, the husband of an old friend who was now searching for me so I would be lobotomized.

As the new leader of Smart City, Sarah had made me public enemy number one. She mistook me for killing her husband and for planning the explosion that harmed fifty innocent civilians. To this day, I was haunted by that reality.

I hoped that someday, somehow, society would know the truth. I would always wish to live a normal life, have kids, and die old; but now I saw that was impossible after what happened. Even if I would find the man in black, how was I going to pick up the threads of an old life? How could I go on when I knew there was no turning back and that all I saw was darkness. The best I could do was find the real killer and make him confess for killing Dr. Barton, along with others, and force him to heal me.

I never asked for this life. But just as I was running away from my family, I was also running away from my friends and even Celia. But no matter how bad it might seem, I would find a way out because even though it was a long shot, it was all that was keeping me going, and not just to survive but also to prove that everybody that hated me to this day were wrong about me and that I was not a mistake, and I would seek justice for the death of Dr. Patrick Barton.

This was January 1, 2024. I was leaving the grave site's fifty poor souls, and some of which I once knew before I took a boat out of Smart City, with the alias of Robert Dent. I had already grown a goatee and cut my hair short, with a few new clothes that were previously from another lifetime that I had inside my backpack. I decided to use these to cover my identity.

I would hope when I escaped, it was not going to be a storm, and I prayed it wouldn't interfere with my quest to find Dr. Patrick Barton's murderer. But now, to this day, what mattered was to run and to keep on running until I made that bastard responsible for destroying my life. I would make him confess for what he'd done, and I refused to go back and get my brain cut open, especially when my own friend thought I killed her husband. I would never give up, and I would never forget until I found the man in black and I knew where the bastard was going. I hoped to find him there to unmask him, make him confess, and cure me of this evil.

I'd be going to Hong Kong, hoping to find him. He was probably working for another crook similar to Linda Smith, but whatever it took, I would find him—hopefully sooner than later.

My name is James David Truman, and I'm a wanted fugitive.

End of Book One

About the Author

Miguel Olmedo was born in Providence, Rhode Island, where he began his early life struggling with mental illness, and he has used his experience with it in the process of writing *City of Anarchy*. Since the year 2012, he is now living a happy and healthy life with his family and has now learned to let go of his past, and he gives thanks to God for giving him a blessed life, and he also thanks his family for believing in him in order to write this book. He also gives his biggest thanks to his grandfather, who believed very much in him, and he would love to dedicate this book to him.

Printed in the USA
CPSIA information can be obtained
at www.ICGtesting.com
LVHW101400030823
754030LV00002B/291